From Here to Argentina

A TANGO LOVE STORY

A NOVELLA BY

Kristina Bak

LUMINARE PRESS

WWW.LUMINAREPRESS.COM

This is a work of fiction. Names, characters, places, and events are either products of the author's imagination, or used in a fictitious manner. Any resemblance to actual persons or actual events is purely coincidental.

From Here to Argentina: A Tango Love Story
© 2017 Kristina Bak

All rights reserved. This book or any portion thereof may not be reproduced or used in any manner whatsoever without the express written permission of the publisher, except for the use of brief quotations in a book review.

Printed in the United States of America

Cover art by Kevin Kadar, represented by
The Froelick Gallery, Portland, Oregon
Cover design by Claire Flint Last

Luminare Press
438 Charnelton St., Suite 101
Eugene, OR 97401
www.luminarepress.com

LCCN: 2017948522
ISBN: 978-1-944733-33-9

*For my daughter, Anna Bak-Kvapil,
who makes everything worthwhile.*

Contents

Lesson One: The Walk 1
Esteban 7
Lesson Two: The Embrace 12
Lesson Three: Valentines 16
Rosalie 25
Lesson Four: Grasshoppers and Ants . . . 29
Lesson Five: The *Cabeceo* 39
Mikhail 43
Roger the Dog 50
The Atlas 58
Howard's End 62
River 69
Lesson Six: Argentine Dreams 73
Body Memory 78
Tango Shoes 88
Staying Alive 91
Lesson Seven: Connection 97
Hot Water 109
Blood Tells 113
Left Early... 120
Girl Talk 130

Easy Come...	134
The Other Side of the Glass	138
Milonga	144
Venus	162
Perfect Sacrifice	167
Don't Cry For Me	174
Acknowledgements	177

Chapter One

Lesson One: The Walk

Rosalie's left leg dazzled Dan. Her muscled calf, her tight thigh disappearing up her skirt, belied what he'd seen of her helpless kitten eyes, yet her ankle was so delicate his hand might fit around it. Rosalie's right leg threatened to distract him, too, as he walked behind her in the circle. Dan looked down at his feet to concentrate on his own steps instead. Their tango teacher counted aloud over the music, *one and two and three and four and…* Before they could dance they must walk, he'd told them; the walk *was* the dance. Dan's tango dreams were slow to transpire with the endless walking, chest up, shoulders relaxed, ankles brushing, no bouncing, rolling on the balls of his feet. Who had imagined how hard this could be?

Dan avoided other students' glances across the room. He knew he was no portrait of poise. He tried to sustain the pace without stepping on Rosalie's heels. They'd all said their names for the teacher at the beginning and Rosalie's was the only one Dan retained. His attention had stalled, stuck on her pink lips as she said it, the *R*'s pout, the widening smile with the *ie*. He'd made a point of getting in line after her.

The class was in a hall rented from the Norwegian Club, and judging from the colored lights still twinkling over the dance floor in these drear post-holiday weeks, the Norwegians appeared to be a jolly bunch. For Dan the decorations were another distraction, a reminder that for him, New Year's Eve hadn't lived up to its giddy promise. The remnant glitter ball hanging from the ceiling suggested that for others, it had. Why would he expect this year to be any better than the last, or the one before that? Only the most persistent optimism brought him here. He craved another human being's touch, and Argentine Social Tango was a dance of close embrace—or it would be, once they'd mastered the walk to their teacher's satisfaction.

Mikhail followed Dan in the circle. Dan's shorter legs and hesitation slowed Mikhail, and he disliked Dan for that, and for having pressured him outside the building. Mikhail had touched the door handle three times, backed away, and was about to try again when the little gray-haired guy nodded to him and went in as though it took no courage at all. Then Dan had held the door open until Mikhail had no choice but to meet his dare. Until that point he could have turned around and gone home, poured a vodka, and taken it to the hot tub on his deck over the river, as he'd done most evenings of his post-divorce transition. His ex said by now it was post-post-divorce malingering, but Mikhail knew he'd been misjudged and treated poorly. His grip on the reins had slipped, and he needed time to get his runaway life back under control.

He'd heard that in tango the men lead and the women follow; that appealed to him. Mikhail felt himself gliding like a tiger now, and Dan was in his way. The circle stuttered and shifted for a late arrival, a woman who introduced herself as Juniper. With an apologetic shrug, she slipped in between Mikhail and Dan. She was over-dressed for a first lesson and over-large for the short, clingy skirt she wore. She moved with more grace than Dan, and Mikhail was happy to follow her.

PART OF TANGO'S APPEAL FOR JUNIPER WAS THE image, all stiletto heels and flirty dresses. She was vexed to see that this crew looked more like a gym class in stocking feet. The dance hall's decorations weren't depressing for her—she kept hers up until Valentine's Day, prolonging the holiday mood. She was drawn to bright, colorful things, convinced that enough beautiful objects collected in one place would, sooner or later, take her life to a tipping point where it, too, would become beautiful, an alchemical process she had yet to perfect.

Her collection leaned toward the cheap and gaudy, not through lack of taste, but through the relative poverty that grated on her more each year. The outdoorsy privileged type flocked to retire in this scenic mountain town, while she descended further into the ranks of the service industry. *Hospitality*, her boss preferred to call their gourmet catering business, but Juniper felt more and more like a servant to her peers. She did her best to distract herself with a fantasy world. Pleasure was her natural element, and she intended tango to be a new facet of that. She would dance like Ginger Rogers if she could find a Fred Astaire.

Rosalie glimpsed Mikhail striding several places behind her. He appeared to be the only man in the room who wasn't hopeless as a potential tango partner. While the others stumped along watching their feet, Mikhail held his head high and rolled heel-to-toe in rhythm with the music, displaying the kind of accuracy and confidence Rosalie liked. He seemed to like himself as well, given the arrogant lift of his thick eyebrows, the set of his mouth. They would look good dancing together, never mind that the top of her head would barely reach his shoulder. She focused on the balls of her feet touching the polished wood floor in perfect alternation, each pushing off with enough energy to carry her fluidly forward, stretching her legs in one long step after another.

She hoped she looked as competent and self-possessed as Mikhail did, and that he was noticing her, too. She didn't have much competition in this group as far as she could see—a couple of nice grandmothers, an insecure twenty-something girl, a white-haired woman obviously bonded to her white-haired husband, and overweight Juniper, who'd made a fuss coming in late, with her frivolous clothing and round, bronze-colored eyes. At first sight, Juniper seemed enviably carefree, off in a fairy world where nothing real impinged. Rosalie was a realist, here for a purpose. She wasn't looking for intimacy, *au contraire*, but training wheels for restarting her life as a widow in this new town. Tango's formality offered safe practice in finding her balance, though now that she'd seen Mikhail, she mused it might offer a bit more.

Esteban (well, Jason, but what kind of name is *Jason* for a tango teacher?) recited their names to himself as he clapped the rhythm. It made them feel special to be called by name, especially the older ones, easier to accept corrections when they sounded warm and personal. He was usually good at learning names and remembering them as long as he needed to, which in his most recent career had been the length of a Caribbean cruise. He should have kept at it. The cruise captain had christened him Esteban, and though he'd had other made-up names, this one stuck. On the ship he'd had a captive audience, all hell-bent on having fun. Who knew how many of this bunch would last the whole eight weeks? The singles, he suspected, were on the prowl, the couples aiming to rekindle some romance.

Very good! Chests up, backs long, strut a little, energy in how your feet meet the floor! Now, ladies, turn around and walk backwards! He needed them to fall in love with tango as he had, to depend on it like a drug. Tango had never betrayed him. His errors lay in trusting the wrong women. The last one left him living in his car in this extortionate Central Oregon ski town, too broke to leave, too broke to stay. Sometimes he felt frightened at his plight; often he felt cramped and cold sleeping in his back seat, his breath freezing on the inside of the windows.

But if love hadn't worked for him yet, that didn't mean it never would. Life is filled with wonderful surprises. Unfortunate things turn out to be brilliant, like when he couldn't afford a haircut, his long dark hair tied in a man-bun made him look like a *telenovela* star, a convincing persona for teaching tango. He posted his photo with an online ad. With money from the students his ad attracted he rented the Norwegian Club hall one evening a week, and bought groceries and gas. By spring, he planned to be half a world away.

Chapter Two

Esteban

There was no bonding that first evening. Everyone left with nothing more than a courtesy smile for Esteban, but he could win them over. He was an actor, after all, or had been—a *has-been* without having actually *been*. He recoiled from remembering his arrival in L.A. twenty years before as a long-lashed, lissome New Jersey boy. After growing up in a place that resembled a black-and-white movie, he was astonished, like Dorothy, to abruptly find himself in Technicolor. Finding himself in any movie would have been the answer to his dreams, and for a while he was so close he could smell it, passed from party to party, a blur of mansions and blue pools, living the life without its substance.

In retrospect he almost admired his stupidity, his ability to flow with sensation and lies, without money, without worry, without doubt, as the pools got smaller, the promises hazier, the parties reduced to white powder up his nose in a stranger's bathroom. One moment he was joyriding through the Hollywood Hills as a passenger in somebody's leased Maserati, the next he was marooned on a curb at the east end of Sunset Boulevard, watching the car roar away and his shadow elongate across the gritty sidewalk in the sunrise.

By then he wasn't so pretty as he used to be, or so much a boy. He cleaned up well enough, though, to start over, to climb the hellish ladder from less-than-no-one to no-one-important. He got roles—if you wanted to call them that—in movies that ranged from execrable to decent. In what was meant to be his great break, he played a waiter to a fairly famous actor in a scene that got cut. That career sank and the cruise ship became his life raft, but he'd abandoned that, too. His one abiding role was playing himself, Esteban, which he did with middling success. This time, if he performed well, Aurelia would be his golden statuette.

The day before Christmas, Esteban had been keeping warm in the downtown library, scrolling through Argentine tango sites on his laptop, killing time—no one to call from his past, no dreams for the future, his present dead in the water—when he came across Aurelia in a teaching video and felt bushwhacked. He knew instantly from the zing he felt that it was fate. He'd been clean for years, or mostly, but she gave him a rush that set his heart pounding before his brain caught up. If her accent made her hard to understand, her voice and her body spoke for themselves. Esteban scoured the web; his obsession grew with each Aurelia sighting. As far as he could tell, she was unattached, always with a different dance partner. If his many other liaisons had collapsed, black holes sucking away his love illusions, not to mention his money, it was for the good: Aurelia had to be his true destiny. Angling for an invitation to Buenos Aires—soon, too, before the southern summer waned—he sent her an email with a video of himself dancing tango on the cruise ship stage. The suspense was agonizing. When she finally had replied, her response lacked the effusiveness his performance merited. Esteban attributed this to the language barrier.

Hola, Esteban. I like for you to come my earliest opening in May, winter season discount, lodgings available near where I teach, and less crowded milongas. Must bring at least two other leads and three follows to reserve class time. Send payment for all by 15 April. (See attached list for cost and informations.)

Hard times in Argentina. He understood she needed paying students, another thing they had in common. He'd take his as a love offering to her, even if he had to sell his car. Once they'd danced together she'd see her error in treating him like a common tango tourist. Soon it would be *Esteban and Aurelia* in those videos. He burned to hold her. He locked the door behind his departing class. Two taps and she danced in miniature on his phone screen, her tiny feet in four-inch heels making saucy embellishments between steps, her dark hair flying around her sharp-boned face with its knowing smile. There in the empty Norwegian Club, his phone held high, Esteban danced across the floor beneath the Christmas lights, imagining himself the man who led Aurelia.

THE CLOSEST ESTEBAN HAD COME TO BUENOS Aires was studying with Alejandro, his first and finest tango *maestro*. Alejandro was a true *milonguero*, authentically sprung from Rio de la Plata, where Argentine Social Tango evolved. When he was barely old enough to walk Alejandro had danced, his baby feet atop his father's, holding his father's hands, to the music of violin and bandoneon. Alejandro's parents had tangoed the night he was conceived; his mother tangoed with him growing in her belly and left the *pista* the evening he was born only when her pains became too severe for her to stand. Alejandro had tango in his cells, in his soul; he breathed tango. By the time Esteban met him, Alejandro was teaching in Santa Monica—with middling looks, and well into middle age, neither tall nor svelte—women of all ages queuing to dance with him, to spend a tanda finding tango nirvana in his arms. He was a happy man who never forgot his roots. Esteban wanted some of that, yet no matter how he worked and practiced, he couldn't achieve the grounded buoyancy that came so naturally to

Alejandro. He never stopped trying. He held to the conviction that someday, with the gravitas of maturity, he would succeed. His youthful sexuality and flashy footwork had gained him a tolerant smile from his teacher. Two decades on, maturity had crept up on Esteban. Perhaps in Argentina he would find his gravitas.

Now, Esteban researched all week, wearing out his welcome in one Wi-Fi café after another, inhabiting a virtual Buenos Aires. He had to convince his students he knew the city and its tango world so they would buy into the tour. He'd watched the cruise ship tour guides in action; it was all about confidence. His accent was good. He'd learned to order dinner or direct a taxi in Spanish with flair, though sometimes triggering a rapid-fire conversation that became quickly one-sided. Esteban downloaded videos of Buenos Aires social dances, *milongas*—the dresses, the heels, the dignified men and elegant women, the atmosphere restrained and erotic. At the next lesson he would give his students a taste to whet their appetites, leave them hungry for more.

Chapter Three

Lesson Two: The Embrace

The class shrank to nine, the walk having washed out a few. With the odd number of students, one follow at a time had to watch from the sidelines as they learned *the embrace, meeting at the heart, becoming the four-legged creature.* When the music stopped, each man moved to the next woman in the circle and one woman traded places with the watcher, so that every follow eventually danced with every lead. The simple system created inordinate confusion, which Esteban showed good humor sorting out. Juniper's first partner was an acrid-smelling twenty-something whose pert girlfriend was paired with Mikhail across the circle.

Mikhail, with his wavy chestnut hair and brooding grace, was the only man in the room who fit Juniper's romantic Argentine dreams, but she found no romance in this evening. With the holiday lights stashed away, the room looked forsaken. A dozen paper snowflakes dangled in their place— Norse juju to lure snow to the mountains, stave off another drought year, and make for good skiing. Beneath the snowflakes each couple leaned chest-to-chest, their hands behind their backs while trying to pin a flat cushion between them as they walked to the music, with much laughter when a cushion dropped. It was like a childhood party game, and Juniper was as quickly bored as she had been at birthday parties when she was small. The point, she gathered, was to help puritanical introverts be comfortable with their upper bodies touching as they danced. Ho-hum.

Dan was good-natured about this easing into intimacy. He hadn't touched a woman in a long time, and he hadn't laughed in a while, either. He did the cushion walk with a bejeweled grandmother and a twenty-year-old in his progress around the circle, looking forward to his turn with Rosalie of the fine legs and sweet lips. When it came, Esteban took away the cushions; Dan hadn't counted on that. Esteban modeled the embrace *apilado*, bodies angled out from sternum to feet, the follow's left arm over the lead's right shoulder, the lead's right arm around the follow's back, free hands clasped at shoulder height.

Rosalie and Dan obeyed instructions and stood embraced, waiting, while Esteban inspected each couple, making adjustments here and there. Rosalie's blond curls tickled Dan's nose. He concentrated on being casual; tango was a dance of passion, but not that kind of passion, at least not in class. Rosalie seemed nonchalant, as though it were easy for her to discount his maleness. She smiled up at him through her mascara. The overhead lights made shadows that hollowed her eye sockets. He fought a sudden unwelcome awareness of the skeleton inside her taut body.

At sixty-eight, Dan didn't see well without his glasses anymore, and Esteban had made him take them off to dance. What he missed with his eyesight disturbed him far less than what he saw with his inner vision. He was outwardly more solid than colorful, each day consumed by inconsequential challenges, waiting for what could go wrong, no day since *that* one standing out much from another. He'd tried alcohol and drugs, then studied Buddhism to learn to live with suffering, because he didn't believe he deserved to live without it. His lessons in the impermanence of all things had worked too well: the knowledge possessed him, awareness run amok. Like the monks who drank their tea from human skulls, he saw death and decay everywhere. It was his curse, a genetic susceptibility, nature *and* nurture. He'd bought an app for his phone hyped to trigger meditation on impermanence. The obsession lodged in his mind permanently, even after he deleted the app. His first embrace of Rosalie threatened to become a *danse macabre*, as if he circled the floor with a corpse in his arms. His vision contracted to a pinpoint; he felt wobbly on his feet.

Esteban shattered the trance with his corrections—Rosalie's arm lighter on Dan's shoulder, Dan's elbow lower, his embrace firmer around Rosalie's slender back. Dan was perplexed by the expectations this imposed on him, to simultaneously experience this woman alive in his arms and to walk her backward in the circular line of dance without treading on her toes. Rosalie was polite about his technique and kept her toes out of his way as they danced. When they changed partners, Dan sank against Juniper with relief. Her softness absorbed his fears, and she had a rich smell that evoked his long-lamented youth. Halfway around the circle with her it came to him: patchouli.

To Esteban the lesson dragged. These students were no worse than others he'd taught, but the point of the evening for him was to pitch them the Buenos Aires tour. Once he'd cracked their initial resistance to the embrace, he couldn't wait. He showed them a *milonga* video. They seemed riveted watching the dancers. Afterwards he flourished his announcement like a magician reading their minds—his personal connection in Argentina, the bargain price, the exceptional opportunity. It wasn't entirely untrue. He noted their reactions to the news. The white-haired couple raised their eyebrows at each other, the twenty-something boy looked nervously away from his girlfriend. Esteban couldn't yet tell about the others.

From Here to Argentina

Chapter Four

Lesson Three: Valentines

Red paper hearts with lacy perforations fluttered from the ceiling, reminding Mikhail of Valentine exchanges in elementary school, "be mine" meaningless on chalky pastel candies. The cutouts stirred his fear that his heart might be riddled with holes, too. He hadn't visited his doctor in years—the man might have retired by now. *Hypochondria* was what he'd said, and even charged Mikhail for the insult. He didn't know why the doctor wouldn't tell him the truth, perhaps because it was too grim.

Esteban had annoyed Mikhail as well, correcting his impression about men and women in tango, saying the *lead* leads and the *follow* follows; the roles weren't gender specific. In Mikhail's tango fantasies they were, and in class Rosalie embodied them, her cheek pressed to his chest, trusting as a child, fragile in his embrace, so light he felt as though he were circling the floor alone. The voluptuous woman named Juniper, who either had been born to hippie parents or misguidedly re-baptized herself, was harder to lead, her presence more aggressive, though she was easy on her feet. Mikhail contemplated his possibilities.

Esteban ran the class through a slapdash review, *walking in the embrace in the parallel system, lead's left foot to follow's right*, and so on. This evening was about seduction, his seducing at least two men and three women to lay out their deposit for the trip to Argentina, padded with his fee as their guide. To do that, he had to show them something wonderful. His butt, for starters, in his tight black jeans, as he demonstrated *ochos*, leading an imaginary partner, then pivoting his upper torso and his hips independently in a follow's figure eights.

Dan watched Rosalie from the corner of his eye. She wore a red knit dress that would have looked suggestive on a larger woman. She wore it with such innocence, it seemed an assault to pay attention to her breasts when she bent to adjust her socks. Dan found Esteban's swiveling at the waist disconcerting. He wasn't sure that he, himself, boasted a waist *to* swivel. No one had warned him it was a requirement for tango. Esteban had a handsomeness Dan couldn't take seriously, like a character in a romance novel, but the women seemed transfixed by his demonstration and his warm voice with the slight, indefinably Latin accent that seemed stronger than usual.

"*Feel* the tango, sixty-four beats a minute, *dos por cuatro*, *POM pom, POM pom*, the rhythm of your heartbeat." *And incredibly sexy*, Esteban hoped his body was communicating, so the men would want to be him and the women want to be with him, and they would all want to go to Argentina, though they would find when they got there they couldn't dance the way he did. He chose di Sarli's *A la Gran Muñeca* for its clear tango beat—two strong, two weak—and set them all walking in the embrace again.

His prospects looked bad with the twenty-something couple, accusing each other when they stumbled. The boy was used to obeying his girlfriend, who was trying to force him into a graceful lead. No chance that way, they had it all wrong. Tango wasn't a tool for dominance. It was about listening to the music and your partner with your whole body, your whole mind, for the length of a three- or four-song *tanda*, then parting with a "thank you," and meaning it. The white-haired married couple was doing rather well; they'd long outgrown struggles for dominance and futile mutual expectations, and he saw the spark in their eyes when he talked up Buenos Aires. They'd taken the hook. After an hour Esteban called a break to reel them in.

Juniper ran into Rosalie in the restroom dabbing under her arms with a tissue. She hadn't thought of Rosalie as someone who would sweat. Rosalie made space for her at the single sink and turned her attention to tidying her eyeliner. Speaking to Juniper's reflection in the mirror as she washed her hands, Rosalie said, "Are you going?"

"Going where?"

"To Argentina, with Esteban. He's very cute. I've seen the way he looks at you."

Juniper would have noticed, and *cute* hadn't been in her vocabulary for guys since middle school. "Maybe." Such a lie. Nice to keep the make-believe going a few more weeks.

"Oh, you should! I think I'll go if Mikhail does. That would be an adventure."

"You think Mikhail is cute, too?"

"Mikhail is gorgeous, and I'll bet barely fifty. Aren't we lucky we're so well preserved?"

By the restroom's stark fluorescents Juniper could see Rosalie was at least ten years older than she was herself, older than she would have guessed on the dance floor, nearing retirement age, if a person could afford to retire. "When I hear *preserved* I think pickles or strawberry jam."

Rosalie fluffed her bangs and laughed uneasily into the mirror.

IN THE EVENING'S SECOND HALF ESTEBAN TAUGHT them *leading to the cross*. To Rosalie it sounded appropriate for the beginning of Lent, though it had nothing to do with *that* cross. She missed her relinquished religion; you could speak your deepest shame and find absolution. *How long has it been since your last confession, my child? Forty-six years, Father.* Perhaps on her deathbed, should she be so blessed as to have one. She caught Mikhail watching her and watched him right back. Their practice partnering was impersonal under Esteban's close supervision, focused on Mikhail's turning his chest to lead Rosalie to cross her left ankle over her right. Still, something passed between them unspoken.

Dan was sitting on the sidelines, tying his shoes after class, when he saw Rosalie and Mikhail leave together, or maybe not *together*, but at the same time. Mikhail held the door wide for Rosalie, letting in a brutal draft. Dan couldn't miss noticing. He caught Juniper looking, too, not even pretending she wasn't, and she looked no more pleased than he was. Dan smiled as though nothing bad had happened. Juniper did the same, pulling on knee-high black boots. They were sexy boots meant to send a signal, Dan guessed. He knew he wasn't the intended receiver, but he might try for second best. He tested his theory. "Would you like to come by my place for a drink?"

Juniper shot another look toward the door where Mikhail and Rosalie had disappeared. "Something warm would be nice. It's arctic tonight."

Dan's apartment, two blocks away on the second floor of a nondescript frame building, was bare and beige inside. Juniper said it looked Zen. The truth was he couldn't find motivation to buy furniture. He slept on a futon in what was meant to be a living room, and he called the bedroom his library, or den, or office, or even dressing room, to suit his need. Dan left their coats on the twin-sized bed that served as his dresser, a warm cat-shaped dent in the pile of clothes folded neatly on top, no cat in sight.

Juniper plopped cross-legged onto the futon and stripped off her boots. Dan didn't think she was being suggestive, given that there were no chairs. He made Irish coffee, though Juniper said she rarely drank. Nor did he, but they agreed to throw caution to the winds. Affable despite neither being the other's companion of choice, they talked about Esteban's tango tour. Dan didn't say he'd move mountains to go to Argentina if Rosalie were going. That might have been hurtful, and he wasn't yet sure it was true. The alcohol went quickly to his head. Juniper asked for a second, and he joined her, not wanting to be rude. He found himself sitting beside her on the futon, leaning on her shoulder, her soothing largeness drawing out his words. "To go or not, it's hard to work out. I always have a committee in my mind, arguing, pointing fingers, like there's a right way and I have to find it, and everyone knows it better and sooner than I do."

Juniper rested her head against Dan's. "Sounds exhausting."

They nuzzled amiably before he dozed off. When he woke around midnight, Juniper was gone. She'd rinsed their two mugs and filled the cat's water bowl before she left.

Mikhail walked Rosalie to where she'd parked, around the block, where pine trees made the street darker than it needed to be. He shouldn't have found her intimidating—she was petite, feminine by his definition—but he heard an insistence in her voice that made him reluctant to get into her car when she invited him. Cold wind biting his neck decided it. He slid onto the leather seat. She started the engine and grinned at him, her eyes and teeth fluorescing before she switched off the dash lights.

"It warms up fast. The seats are heated."

"Nice car."

"Thanks." Rosalie fondled the steering wheel. "The first car I ever chose myself. I bought it after my husband died."

Mikhail was pleased she was a widow. The divorcees he'd met were always angry; no matter what he did it seemed he wore a hologram of the man who'd done them wrong. He hoped the jerk his ex was dating got the same treatment from her. She'd driven Mikhail to desperate acts, but she didn't see things that way. "I'm sorry. For your loss, I mean."

"He was much older than me. He had a bad heart."

Mikhail didn't want to think about that. After all, a wonky heart wasn't contagious. Being with Rosalie couldn't make his any worse, though he felt a tremor when she laid her right hand on his knee. He had to lean toward her to hear what she was saying. His ear was bad on that side, and her voice was pitched soft.

"I like the way you dance."

"I've always been good. When I was a boy my parents made us kids take Russian folk dance classes. All the sibs hated it, except me, the baby, so they hated me, too."

Rosalie massaged his thigh. "Surely they didn't *hate* you, Mikhail!"

"Oh, they did. Ours was a sizeable family, eleven kids."

"Eleven!" Rosalie seemed to be ignoring her working hand creeping up his leg, so Mikhail tried to, too.

"By the time I came along the affection was mostly used up. Everything was. I never know for sure if what I remember belongs to me, or if it's some hand-me-down from the older kids."

"One of the benefits of being an only child, I don't have to remember anything I don't want to."

"It's warm in here now." Mikhail was sweating beneath his jacket. He was sure he smelled. He hadn't expected this from Rosalie, wasn't absolutely sure she wanted what she seemed to want, and he needed to take a piss. He tried to distract himself with conversation. "Did you and your husband dance?"

Rosalie jerked her hand back, and hugged herself inside her coat. "Before."

"Before what?"

"Before the stroke."

"I thought it was his heart?"

"That, too. He went quickly, saved us the indignity of watching each other grow old." She turned the car lights back on. "It's late, I'd better go. I'll see you in class next week."

Mikhail was hardly out of the car, raising his collar against the wind, when Rosalie drove off.

Chapter Five

Rosalie

Sometimes Rosalie wished she'd grown up ugly, obliged to rely on herself, not taken underwing by a man for whom possession was ninety percent of marriage. True, she'd begun without much promise. A colicky infant at the bottom of the developmental graph, she grew into a slight, colorless child, easily overlooked and obedient. Her parents were mild suburban people, mildly chagrined at their sole offspring's lack of vigor. When it came time for school she disliked the rowdy boys and girls who taunted her diffidence at recess. Those were the days Red Rover and Dodge Ball channeled "healthy aggression" on the playground. Bullying was the natural privilege of the strongest and meanest, though never named.

Rosalie wasn't strong or mean, but she was smart. She begged her parents for a puppy, and when they gave in she chose her canine ally with care. Sir Lancelot wasn't the friendliest puppy in his litter. Rosalie didn't want friendly—she wanted a puppy who would grow to have big ears to listen for her commands, and big teeth to carry them out. She read everything she could find about dogs and shared every free moment from breakfast to bedtime with her German Shepherd. He became her best friend, her weapon, the sibling she never had, the robust alter ego she carried in her psyche.

Her Grandmother Meares had told her about their second-, or third-, or whatever-once-removed cousin, Cecil, a dog handler and Russian interpreter on the British Terra Nova expedition to the South Pole. The expedition ended with death and failure in 1913, but Cecil had had the good sense to leave in 1912. Rosalie wondered if the predilection for canine companionship, and survival, flowed in her blood. As with all dog stories, Lance's ended too soon for Rosalie, though he died at a fine old age in dog years. He left her sweet grief, and a marketable skill. She earned college tuition in Santa Barbara walking dogs and pet-sitting for problem animals. The confused creatures found solace in her understanding, and their owners found reassurance in her advice. Her talent generalized across feline and equine realms, but she reserved her greatest love for dogs.

She met Howard the summer his Rottweiler went into decline, not surprisingly reflecting Howard's own disorientation at his first real defeat, stung by his wife's defection at forty. When Rosalie's curls brushed her delicate shoulders as she knelt nose-to-nose with Caesar, she became the solution to Howard's predicament, along with his dog's.

Rosalie found Howard lovable in a virile, blunt-spoken way, qualities he cultivated as a litigator for those too wealthy to be famous. He was old enough to be her father, but the similarity ended there. Howard cherished her as he did all his favorite objects. When the priest said, *Do you, Howard Walter Howards, take Mary Rosalie Meares to have and to hold,* he took the vow literally, lifted her from the student scrum directly into the privileged life her college friends aspired to, and kept her, a collaborator in her own captivity. Whenever her professional ambitions stirred, Howard diverted her with trips to Las Vegas or Paris or Monte Carlo.

Howard's three children each had a room in their homes on both coasts, homes which grew grander with his reputation. Rosalie tried to treat the children as her own, taking the bumpy ride through their adolescent agonies with all the compassion she could generate, lacking memories of their sweet innocent years to sustain her. She tried especially hard with the youngest child, the girl. They shopped or went for runs on the beach. His sons were more difficult for her to understand. She plied them with food and movies on the many custodial weekends and holidays that Howard was embroiled in a case. When the children went home to their mother, Rosalie teased Howard about making a baby of their own. He would caress her flat, firm belly and tell her no one needed to reproduce more than he had.

Now, alone in the world, she tried to emulate Howard's pattern, which had held her in his protective custody all her adult life. Her entire way of being had been colonized by Howard's dominance. From the day they'd met she'd absorbed his techniques for overmastering doubts, counteracting inclinations of anyone who opposed his goals. He'd been direct in his demands, refusing to consider they might be denied or delayed. Rosalie didn't understand why she'd failed in the simple seduction of Mikhail. She wondered if it was because she wasn't certain herself exactly what she wanted. Not the way Howard had been.

Chapter Six

Lesson Four: Grasshoppers and Ants

As Esteban could have predicted, the young couple bickered through the fourth lesson. He doubted they'd be back. Esteban blamed himself for moving the class too rapidly. His efforts had backfired with them—or he could see it as winnowing out the chaff, leaving him to concentrate on his best prospects. He'd closed the deal with the white-haired married couple, who'd come this evening with check in hand. Now that they'd paid the deposit they would work hard on the basics. They'd make a decent, if unspectacular, impression on Aurelia, and be able to benefit from her teaching. He didn't care which of the two remaining men signed on. Mikhail, the better dancer, seemed high maintenance; Dan would be an easier fellow traveler.

Esteban had learned to read male character as self-defense, growing up the middle, and smallest, of three brothers. His mother had consigned him to fraternal purgatory in their carpeted basement rec room, where he was fair game for any torture that didn't leave marks. He soon learned that worse than pain inflicted by the bigger boys was punishment for bearing tales about it with no physical proof. His mother was a sweet, scholarly woman of refined tastes who'd given birth three times, longing for a daughter. She relied on her husband to interpret and restrain their sons' barbarism and remove them from the house whenever possible. This meant weekend football games and fishing trips that couldn't have bored Esteban more. For his own preservation he became the family comedian, clowning to defuse tense situations. He wasn't particularly good at it, but as the best act in the family he made his mother laugh.

Esteban's domestic acting success skewed his self-image in ways that hadn't necessarily served him well in the long run. And he wasn't such a good judge of women. He needed two more for Argentina. The married couple's elderly friend, diamonds weighting her crinkled earlobes, had seemed a good prospect, but she'd resisted his charms and come only twice. That meant he had to entice both Rosalie and Juniper. The class seemed subdued tonight, not an atmosphere favorable to success for his plan. He would spice up the next lesson with the *cabeceo*, the look a *tanguero* gave to invite a woman to dance. He was sure none of his students had a clue what effort he was putting out for them.

Juniper got desperation vibes from Esteban. One eyelid twitched and his glance skipped from face to face. She was sensitive to desperation, though she didn't own it anymore, or it didn't own her. Desperation meant being down to your last hopes, and hope meant expecting something from the future, learning nothing from the past. Perhaps a slow learner, Juniper wasn't stupid. Being without hope, nothing was a disappointment, though sometimes she slipped up on that. She did her best to live for the moment, within reason. Some hopes were trifling enough to sidle into the space between moments and ambush her. Often, desire bulldozed through and she had a hard time recollecting herself afterwards. She'd felt no desire for Dan last week in her tipsy urge to console him. Though he had all his hair, it had gone gray, and honestly, she just didn't feel the chemistry. She doubted he recalled she'd held him and rocked him to sleep on his futon like a mother.

Juniper had walked home from Dan's apartment through the freezing night and run herself a hot bath with sandalwood-scented bubbles. She finished off a leftover lemon layer cake right there in the tub—far more erotic than kissing Dan had been, another sweet moment in her wasted life. Next incarnation, she'd do better. Having recognized her fundamental mistake, she couldn't just thank the universe for the lesson and bow out. Her life force was too strong, it condemned her to go on and on until it was over, though honestly, her heart wasn't in it. She saw others her age suddenly with grandchildren and second homes, retirement incomes, professional accomplishment, and devoted husbands, while she was living paycheck to paycheck in serial monogamy.

She woke one morning realizing she was over fifty and alone, doors closing around her. She was like the grasshopper in the fable. She'd never wanted to be an ant, plugging away at a boring job in a boring suburb with a boring husband for the sake of retiring someday. She'd seen the obvious moral when she first heard the story read to her class in second grade, confusing as it was to have the teacher draw the opposite message from it. Some grasshopper types she knew had done well for themselves, proving you *can* have pretty much everything. She had to keep fiddling.

She was weary of taking care of herself, shopping in consignment stores, cutting her own hair. Her ex-husband's wife saw her as pitiful and sent her unsold seconds from her Las Vegas boutique, which tilted her wardrobe toward flashy and did nothing for her self-esteem. Juniper's life was her ongoing work of art, without financial value, as ephemeral as the meals she helped cater. Tango was a new flourish for it, something to add flavor.

Flavor, spice, excitement, and—after too many

Puget Sound rainy seasons—sun, were what she'd been looking for when she finished high school and left home. Juniper had hitchhiked south, which in the late 70s was a more iffy proposition than it was in her childhood, when she and her fey mother had done a good deal of it. Why pay bus fare, her mother had said, when I have this thumb? Juniper abided by that wisdom, but, stranded in a windstorm near Dinosaur, Colorado, dehydrated and half-blinded, she was doubting it when a VW Bug emerged from blowing sand on the empty highway as though sent just for her. The woman behind the wheel was sun-bleached and wiry, on her way to the Green River, where she managed camp and cooked for river-rafters. She said she could use a helper. Everything about her proclaimed adventure and freedom. You had to be tough in the macho atmosphere, she told Juniper, but if she hung in, the guys would accept her. Juniper was strong and fearless in those days, and stubborn, too. It didn't hurt that besides being big, she was also at the height of her youthful beauty. She caught the guide fraternity's attention long enough to learn the job and prove her worth.

Juniper resisted rules imposed by other people. The river rules were different: you followed them or you died. The water could suck you under, roll you around, spit you out—the drama suited her. She pitied her peers stuck in mundane jobs and classrooms. The tourists brought myriad emotions to their floats down the Green, not least, a gratifying admiration for Juniper. Two months into her new career she met Greg.

Neither their marriage nor its demise were foreseen when Juniper and Greg were starting out as rafting guides on the Green, the Rogue, the John Day, the Owyhee, and most anywhere else they could be paid for doing what they loved to do. Their bodies fell in love first, flawless and tanned, riding rapids beneath the sun, and each other at their camps' far edges in the dark. They were both surprised it didn't end with the season, as most river romances did. Their one shared interest was river running, which sustained them through their twenties, when they could live on air and adrenaline as long as they had a place to unroll their sleeping bags at night. As they acquired a few things, their differences began to show. Juniper brought books on their rafting trips and signed up for college in the winter. Greg's one professional goal was to never have to work indoors.

That she'd come out of their marriage smelling like a rose was an irony she could never share. Greg was a decent guy. He felt almost as bad as she did about his leaving her, and since Glory, his second wife, had stolen him but was otherwise a decent person herself, Juniper had the benefit of Glory's guilt feelings, too.

Juniper and Greg were both thirty when he took a job guiding a Grand Canyon trip. For the first time since they'd known each other, she stayed behind in Eugene. Summer classes would put her over the top for an English degree, which would get her exactly where, she wasn't sure. She found sporadic work tutoring kids in reading.

While Greg was gone she had more time to herself than she wanted. She wouldn't allow the word *lonely* to surface: it seemed pathetic and she didn't see herself that way. Eugene was half-empty between university terms, and blowsy with heat. Juniper might have enjoyed peaceful hours reading on the porch swing with an iced tea at hand, if not for the daily remodeling din next door. She felt the carpenters eyeing her every morning returning from her run, and she watched them from behind her curtains. Greg often worked construction between guiding jobs. It was comforting to have familiar-looking bronzed bodies next door.

A week into the job, a new man joined the crew. She noticed him because he was fine-drawn, with red hair like a flame. Tattoos webbed his body from neck to waist, maybe lower. Juniper went outside to water her dahlias and lettuces. If anyone had asked, she would have denied that she brushed her hair and changed clothes first. She'd neglected her garden for too long. Juniper spent enough time weeding to need to bring out a pitcher of lemonade around lunchtime. She could never later reconstruct how their conversation began across the neighbor's driveway, or how it happened that while the others drove off to eat somewhere else, the red-haired man ended up in a lawn chair in the shade beneath her striped umbrella. He was a non-stop talker, irreverent, narcissistic, Juniper engrossed in the subtext. When they went inside to make him a sandwich, he picked up the guitar Greg was perpetually messing with and proved his claim to be a musician true, even modest. His said his name was Dakota, just Dakota.

The second day Juniper harvested raspberries warm from the noontime sun, and they shared them with whipped cream. Dakota's presence in her kitchen didn't bear too much examination. He'd been born, contrary to his name, in Alaska, and he distracted her from asking herself why she'd invited him in with his wilderness tales, some of which sounded unlikely. When she questioned them, he ended the conversation with music that mesmerized her like a cobra to its charmer's flute. Dakota looked into her eyes as he played. She felt his fingers on the vibrating strings as though they strummed down her vertebrae beneath her cotton dress. When Juniper tried to read later that afternoon, the words swam off the page.

The third day he came for lunch, they went straight to bed. Both salty with sweat, they slid over and under each other with an abandon Juniper had never felt with Greg. Dakota asked for a beer afterwards and lay propped against the pillows, drinking it and wolfing his sandwich while Juniper traced his tattoos with her fingers—dragons and brambles, skin between them luminescent where his clothes protected it from the sun, so sensitive her mouth left red marks like bruises.

His lunch break was short. The next two days Dakota skipped the sandwich altogether in favor of sex and more beer. Juniper didn't protest that he needed to eat; she loved that he feasted on her. He watched her as he did, and insisted she keep her eyes open, too, *so you know who you're with*. Dakota promised he'd make a new song about her. Juniper was under no illusion he'd stay when the project was finished. He didn't feel real to her; he was a chimera pieced from her fantasies. He'd be safely gone before Greg was due. Meanwhile, she couldn't get enough of him. That last time, she took a book to her porch swing as a decoy when he went back to work. She watched him climb a ladder, balancing a two-by-four, his hips undulating, his last step missing the top rung by a slipshod inch.

Dakota pinwheeled off the ladder like a circus acrobat without a net. He struck the ground near Juniper's raspberry trellis. At first it looked as though he'd got the wind knocked out of him. Like a freeze-frame scene, no one moved: even the butterflies seemed suspended over the garden until Juniper screamed. Everything happened quickly then: sirens and firemen and Dakota hauled away by EMTs. The construction crew downed tools and followed in their pickups. As the last siren waned, a hummingbird zipped past Juniper's ear, a bumblebee droned. After a while she went inside and put Dakota's beer bottles in the recycling bin.

Chapter Seven

Lesson Five: The Cabeceo

The Norwegians, in a fit of hyper-efficiency, had replaced the red hearts with shamrocks weeks before Saint Paddy's Day. The glossy four-leaf clovers suggested to Esteban that his luck might change, though his mother's people were Welsh, and he knew true shamrocks had three leaves, just as he knew St. Patrick had been born in Wales, not Ireland. Some things were certain, mostly those things he'd learned from his mother as a child. Six students had shown up tonight, the twenty-somethings having disappeared. At least they made an even number, follows and leads, eager to work. Esteban reviewed the earliest things he'd taught them—posture, the walk, a proper embrace—and let errors pass without comment. Feeling generous, he thought they were all doing fairly well, except that Mikhail was leading Rosalie like she was a wheelbarrow full of cement.

At their turn to partner, Mikhail had gotten Rosalie's impersonal smile, like one from a cheerleader, or a doctor about to give an injection. He guessed she was punishing him for his aloofness at the previous week's class. He'd felt nervous with her then, spooked by their conversation in the car, though that didn't stop his remembering her hand hot on his thigh through his jeans. Tonight her shoulders felt rigid in his embrace as they danced, clumsy in steps they'd both mastered by the third lesson. Was she willfully making him look bad? Mikhail fought his anger. He didn't know her well enough yet to be sure.

Juniper scrolled through nonexistent messages on her phone during the break. She didn't want to encourage Dan to expect another tête-à-tête. She noted whatever Rosalie had going with Mikhail didn't appear to have progressed too far—Rosalie was taking refuge in the restroom, Mikhail drinking from a water bottle with his back to them all. Esteban cornered Dan, probably to wheedle him into the tour. Juniper was considering turning off her phone and trying for a real conversation with Mikhail when Rosalie reappeared and took the chair beside her.

"Texting your boyfriend?"

"I wouldn't be here alone if I had one."

"Me neither. I thought this would be a fun way to meet men."

"Isn't it?"

"These two?"

"There's always Esteban."

They giggled like best friends.

With ten minutes left in the lesson, Esteban sent the men and women to separate sides of the room. "In Argentine tango you invite a partner by the *cabeceo*—full-frontal eye contact. The lead looks across the room directly at the chosen follow, the follow returns the look, perhaps a nod—*Yes*—and they meet on the dance floor. Or, perhaps the follow turns away: *No*, or *Not right now*. No one knows but the two of you, so no one loses face, no walk of shame for the rejected. Follows can initiate the *cabeceo*, too. If you don't look, you don't dance. We'll practice now for when we go to Buenos Aires." The *when* was no slip of the tongue.

Esteban started di Sarli's *A la Gran Muñeca*, strong on the bandoneon and lush violins, with a clear beat. He dimmed the lights, the shamrocks winking green reflections. The *cabeceo* could be hard for the shy. At least the married couple seemed to be having fun with it, ogling each other. Both other leads were staring at Rosalie.

Rosalie accepted Dan. She was struck by the kindness of his embrace. He seemed grateful to have her in his arms, and gentle, as though he were afraid she might not survive a tighter grip. His white shirt smelled freshly laundered. She'd scarcely registered her turns with him earlier, tense with her internal battle between irritation with, and attraction to, Mikhail.

Juniper caught Mikhail's eye. She didn't suppose he was the nicest man, but he came in a delicious package, smooth skin, eyes that crinkled when he smiled, and taller than she was. No harm in tasting the fruit, especially if Rosalie didn't want it, and in the dance she was innocent as long as she held the proper embrace—axis aligned, no contact below the sternum. She let her cheek touch Mikhail's jaw, her shoulders wrap him more roundly. He led her in the basic steps Esteban had taught them, and they moved easily in tandem, immersed in the music.

She dawdled on the way home. The night air carried a greening scent she'd forgotten in the clean, cold winter, of catkins on willows bordering the river, evoking an eventual spring. Mikhail pulled alongside in a powder-blue Camry, an oddly domestic choice for him. He lowered the car window. "Want a ride home?"

Juniper kept moving, to not seem too easy. "I live by the park, across the footbridge. I like to walk."

Mikhail drove slowly beside her. "You can walk some other night."

Chapter Eight

Mikhail

Mikhail felt more confident with Juniper than with Rosalie. Juniper sent clear messages, a sensual woman, uncomplicated and available, traits a man could appreciate. He'd learned from his earliest years to take any opportunity for good things that came his way. Mikhail remembered his upbringing as cruel, and to his regret, he remembered it often. He thought at fifty-four childhood would be so far behind him none of it would matter, but it attached to him like a dragon tail that grew longer and heavier each year.

As the eleventh baby, he'd been another obstacle to his mother's rest, like an annoying pet you stumble over when you turn around. His family photo album was inert by his birth. He'd studied photos taken before he was born, trying to catch his family by surprise, hunting for some inkling among them that he would be coming to make them complete, finding only his absence. Moira complained that he'd never become an adult, that their daughters were more mature than he was from the time they were out of diapers. That was one reason she'd given for leaving him.

Already several of his eldest siblings had died. They weren't a long-lived breed. He'd gone to the funerals, shaken hands, bowed his head at condolences for sorrow he didn't feel. Or did he? Was that the pain embedded in his heart? It had taken up residence not long after his mother's passing. He preferred that term—more just going away. That didn't feel strange. It seemed to him his parents were gone before he left for college. Though they'd been alive, there was an expanse of grandchildren and religious difference between him and them that he found impossible to negotiate.

By the time he had babies to contribute, most of their cousins were past puberty and his parents had died. Now he had to name off his brothers and sisters, counting on his fingers to be certain who was left. They were more like aging distant cousins, some of whom he barely recognized the rare times they met. The sister he'd liked best, maybe even loved, and who had been kind to him, didn't know him or anyone else anymore. She'd called him *Papa* in a meek voice when he visited her care home, and he'd never gone back. Each death in his family was proof that things would never be made right, no one would apologize for the thousand injuries they'd inflicted upon him. Moira told him he imagined things, it couldn't have been that bad. She was wrong.

A few had come to his wedding in Portland in a show of family solidarity, condescending to their baby brother who, when they bothered to notice him at all, they found a dim star in their constellation. He'd borrowed from most of them, just until he got on his feet—which he never did, though Moira's family was old money in West Coast terms, a couple of generations. She was Episcopalian, anathema to his mother. She wasn't particularly beauteous, even as a bride showing the slightly slumped shoulders and thin hair that would become more pronounced over time. They began well enough, building their riverside dream home at the end of a long lane on a wooded five-acre lot east of the Cascades and celebrating the birth of their perfect twin girls.

Moira had generous lips that were either her best or her worst feature, depending on whether they smiled at Mikhail with open adoration after their engagement, or pursed in outright rancor as his promises gradually unraveled. He kept up a dutiful lust for her until the fantasies featuring the flirtatious girls in the high school math classes he taught could no longer sustain him in the dark. Moira made patient efforts. He felt her rebuke while he blamed her for his failures. It made sense that he found satisfaction outside the marriage. He was a man, after all, and he worked among women, colleagues and mothers, a remarkable number of whom were equally aggrieved by the marriages they'd made. None of his affairs lasted long. Whether or not by his choice, this pleased him.

When exactly Moira transitioned from devoted spouse to harridan was hard to say; it began around the time she finished law school and their twins were in eighth grade. Both girls were hot-tempered high achievers who squabbled fiercely between themselves. He'd adored his babies and basked in their worship. However disappointing others might find him, in their eyes he was all good, all-powerful. They turned in unison against their father as soon as they were old enough to understand the rumors. They never accused him to his face—they worked on their mother until she did.

He denied everything. The marriage survived a few more tenuous years, but he'd lost the solace of his daughters' trust and, with it, belief in himself. About that time, Mikhail caught his buddy, the soccer coach, transgressing the boundaries between fantasy and illegality, outstripping inappropriate with the star of the girls' team. They both begged him to say nothing, and he might not have. She was, after all, seventeen-and-three-quarters and bound for a sports scholarship.

Mikhail had never tampered with the nubile flesh arrayed row-upon-row in his classroom, teenage girls naive behind their knowing gloss, testing their sexual powers against the constraint of the handsome math teacher who couldn't entirely control his eyes. He refused to admit to himself that he was driven more by envy than by righteous indignation to whisper a few words about the coach to the principal. He couldn't have known they would detonate into a scandal that would make him a whistle-blowing hero until someone leaked his exploits in the staff room in revenge, and trashed his teaching career along with his marriage. There were death threats, graffiti, sabotage, key scratches on his red Miata, a brief Facebook shitstorm. Moira alternated between derision and hysteria. She had no sympathy for him when he badly needed it—those endless nights he lay watching the moon retreat beyond the bedroom skylight and the sun return to stab through it.

His doctor gave him pills. One day, he woke from their sublime pharmaceutical blankness galvanized with a plan. He revved his Miata in the garage and wondered how fast it could go from zero into the thickest pine tree at the far end of their lane. Moira had the decency to call 911 after he found out.

Mikhail came home from the hospital to discover gaps in every room, spaces that furniture and books and his wife and daughters used to fill. Moira had left him her ten-year-old Camry, a bland car she knew he didn't like, and taken the Miata's replacement. His rage was ineffectual, his body feeble. He couldn't wreak the destruction the situation called for. He sat amid the emptiness and cried fat Russian tears over vodka straight from the bottle.

His house grew more disordered. He bought groceries less from appetite than for the checkers' cordial words and their occasional touch when cash was exchanged. For longer than he could later recall, he rarely spoke to anyone else until the dog wandered in, astray or abandoned in the surrounding woods. It was a patient creature, a mutt, middle-aged like himself, a shaggy shepherd mix. He named it Boris. Boris was a good listener. Mikhail poured out his accumulated bitterness and dammed-up frustration until they both grew bored with it. They watched a lot of TV.

Moira paid him alimony, partly from whatever pity survived in her stone heart but mostly to coerce him into steering clear of her and their daughters. He pretended to himself he avoided them by choice. He meant his dependence on Moira's funds to be short-term, though it had already extended alarmingly, and he wanted to buy a new car. His Miata remained crumpled against the tree in the lane, a cautionary reminder that the world is vicious and uncaring; enemies might descend at any time.

Mikhail had felt himself sinking into another zero state. He needed to meet a new woman. The thought of a singles' club made his skin crawl, hungry people ready to pounce on and devour one another, anything better than no one at all. He was about to sign up for skiing lessons when he saw the tango class ad. Like a breaker switch thrown, Mikhail felt his life ignite. He badly needed to reassert his strength, and he'd always been strong on the dance floor. Now, here was this woman, Juniper, presenting herself to him like a gift in gaudy wrap. He wondered if it was time to tow the wreck.

Chapter Nine

Roger the Dog

Dan and Rosalie left the fifth class together, more or less by coincidence, exchanging trivialities about the *cabeceo*. They paused in the parking lot. Tango music came from inside the hall where they'd left Esteban. The cutting cold had retreated. Rosalie, new in town, believed spring's promise. "At last!"

Dan wasn't so easily fooled. "We'll have snow again, sometimes even on the Fourth of July."

"You're joking. That can't be true."

He was sorry he'd said it. He read dismay in her voice, along with disbelief. He'd lost credibility, and dashed her hopes at the same time. Well done.

Rosalie fished keys from her bag. "Can I ask you a big favor? Come with me to walk my dog? I didn't have time before class, and I'm nervous in the dark."

So he hadn't entirely blown it. Dan rode in Rosalie's immaculate Lexus rather than let her see the unwashed old Outback he drove, cars being another item that had lost appeal for him. He didn't want anything to diminish him in her eyes yet, though diminishment was inevitable. Let him be near her for a while first—he could allow himself that.

Rosalie drove with confidence and precision. She lived a mile toward the mountains in a gated community that took some starch out of Dan's pride at being worthy protector. The odds were against her being attacked in its landscaped streets. What Dan lost in pride, he recovered in believing this was Rosalie's way of asking to know him better.

DAN HAD NEVER BEEN A DOG MAN, THOUGH HE'D promised his boys a retriever. He regretted he'd never fulfilled that promise; a large furry golden might have made all the difference. Rosalie's snorting bulldog, Roger, wasn't likely to win him over. It *was* darker in her neighborhood, without the streetlights that disempowered the night in town. Illuminated house numbers lit the curving sidewalk at knee level at each driveway. Rosalie held Dan's arm as they walked. Roger's backside, bouncing along bow-legged in front of them with its jauntily flaunted anus, neutralized the gesture's romance for him. Rosalie didn't seem to notice. "Everyone I've met here is from somewhere else, Dan. What about you?"

Dan savored hearing her say his name while he scrabbled through the permissible parts of his memory to come up with something he could share. "I retired here a few years ago. I was a personal chef for a corporate exec."

"A chef!"

Dan wasn't sure whether he'd impressed or amused her. "I wasn't exactly a culinary artist. My employer had prosaic tastes. He hated anything foreign."

"And where did you live?"

"Oh, Istanbul, Karachi, Kiev, Helsinki." He toned it down. "Chicago, for a while."

"How fascinating!" She was giving him the kitten eyes.

Roger stopped them for a copious urination and, after nosing around, squatted for the rest of what he'd come to do. Dan waited, not looking as Rosalie did unpleasant things with a plastic bag. It wasn't an image he wanted to have of her. He held Roger's leash while she detoured to a rubbish bin, and felt as relieved as Roger looked when the whole episode was over and they headed back.

Rosalie's house was a new mid-century modern, spare-lined and architect-designed like the other houses in her enclave, landscaped with native forest plants and rocks placed to look as though they'd always been there. A tactful wall plaque in the slate-floored foyer thanked him for removing his shoes, which was no hardship—he'd grown up doing that, and he always wore his best socks to tango class. They waded into white carpet. A classically minimal leather chaise, glass tables, and tubular steel side chairs were arranged with an orderliness Dan felt safe inside, everything under control as long as he understood the rules. He looked for somewhere to put his jacket. Rosalie took it from him and hung it in the entry closet. Seeing their jackets side-by-side there gave him a frisson that was almost sexual.

Everywhere Rosalie moved became like a painting, perfectly lit and composed, her as the subject. Not Vermeer, the light was more sfumato, like Leonardo's *Saint Anne* before its restoration, once Dan's favorite painting in the Louvre. Roger the Dog made the single discordant note. The kitchen off the great room gleamed with deluxe appliances and tools. Dan was visualizing cooking there with Rosalie until she opened her fridge, revealing takeout containers in sparse, evenly spaced ranks.

She poured them glasses of Oregon pinot noir and brought a bowl of pitted olives to the coffee table by a sofa facing the fireplace. She patted the cushions, inviting Dan to sit beside her. He couldn't have devised a more ideal scenario, though he might have found the red wine sadistic in a more calculating person, given that the broad sofa, like the carpet, spread pristine as new snow.

Dan anchored his toes in the carpet and balanced his glass. "Your place is more elegant than I'm used to these days, and the wine is better, too."

"I design interiors. I've been my own best client since I moved here. Nothing you see is from before."

Dan took in the room with a new eye. It felt

like being inside Rosalie's brain. He wanted to know what was in her dark corners, the closed rooms, private places. Everyone had a messy spot. That thought had too many layers too difficult to control. Sitting close to her here was more arousing than holding her in tango class. He had never been good at the next move—his arm casually across the seat back, his hand brushing a woman's shoulder, all tended to be lost in indecision or careless words.

"What did you leave behind?" Like that. Too late to unsay it. He understood the geographic cure, the irresistible desire to physically flee the past, and that it generally failed.

Rosalie ate an olive with indifferent finesse, accustomed to being the most beautiful woman in the room, a slam-dunk alone with Dan. She thought for the thousandth time someone should come out with a gas fireplace that added a wood fire's crackling and popping. Probably someone had and was manufacturing it in China. Was there anything a person could want that some entrepreneur wasn't willing to supply? The dilemma lay in figuring out other people's desires. She wasn't equipped to understand reticence, and she'd been indiscreet with Mikhail. Men were full of fears. If she'd taken it slower, it would be Mikhail lifting his glass to her now. Her inner dialogue sounded petulant. That attitude was something she could improve about herself so that her personal fire could burn brighter—a bad metaphor with Dan hovering like a worshipful moth. She needed her admirers to thrive. There was much Dan didn't need to know; Rosalie had gotten rid of all the furniture with stories.

She had always had a singular relationship with chairs, lamps, paperweights. Howard discouraged her pet-whispering career as he did anything that interfered with his plans for the two of them, so she never divulged that supposedly inanimate objects also spoke to her. He seldom noticed Rosalie's experiments in lighting and color and style in their homes. She found her first clients through the more observant of his. Howard couldn't object when they consulted her; she helped them gratis while they paid his exorbitant fees. When they sent their friends, and friends of friends, she started her enterprise.

Traveling with Howard she'd collected textiles and furniture and ideas while he was in meetings or, as she suspected later, private rooms of exclusive casinos. *Architectural Digest* did a write-up on her work that Howard couldn't help noticing—a room he'd been in too many times, the bedroom of an elite client, a woman unnamed and invisible in the photos. Rosalie epitomized discretion. Howard had to play along with kudos that flowed his way for his talented wife's success. Rosalie revealed a talent for business as well as for design, and poured her profits back into her work. She hadn't been raised rich, and the discovery that money made more money intoxicated her. Howard laughed at her naiveté and insisted she let him manage her investments to safeguard her from herself.

She studied Dan. The urge to confess everything was strong. If it were just this companionable hour she might find relief in it, deniability, but there he would be next week at tango, and probably the next, with the off chance they'd end up in Buenos Aires together, too.

"My husband challenged his strength, and mine, constantly. Three years ago we climbed Kilimanjaro. We had a grueling flight back to New York. I was unpacking our bags when I heard a crash. He'd collapsed—couldn't walk, couldn't talk, could barely move one arm. After a week the specialists let him come home with round-the-clock nursing. That Friday night the weekend nurse cancelled. I thought I could manage. I knew the routine, the medication schedule, I'd learned how to do all the necessary things. I hadn't counted on the fatigue. Sunday evening I lay down in my room for a few minutes' rest. When the nurse woke me it was Monday morning, and he was…" Rosalie found she couldn't say the word. "He hadn't rung the bell beside his bed, or if he had, I'd slept through it."

The story came out like an exhibit encased in glass, each word polished and placed in its permanent location. Rosalie produced genuine tears at the end, moved by Dan's pats on her wrist. She felt his touch as a benediction. The version she'd told didn't reflect that badly on her, and she wouldn't tarnish it by badmouthing her late husband. Dan didn't need to know about the financial mayhem that had befallen her as soon as Howard was gone. Or how her stepchildren had turned on her like hyenas for what little was left. Or the other thing.

Chapter Ten

The Atlas

Mikhail made a point of knowing more about others than they knew about him without their noticing. One look inside Juniper's cottage behind her landlord's much larger house told him she had lived alone for some time. Without intervention she would eventually die an old lady buried in tchotchkes, half-eaten by her cats—two, as he could tell by the two food bowls, two water bowls, and two litter boxes stuffed under what could be her dining table, if it weren't stacked with sketchpads, potted plants, library books, used gift wrap, unopened bills, a cat chow bag, and a high-heeled shoe. Nothing in the house suggested a male presence, unless one cat was a tom.

Juniper shed her coat on a chair and sat on it to peel off her black leather boots. She did it brusquely, without exploiting the act's inherent erotic potential. Mikhail found her all the sexier for that, an earthy woman without pretension, no need to figure her out. She dumped unfolded laundry off a yellow sofa for him. "Are you hungry? I'm always starved after tango."

Cat hair clung to Juniper's fluffy socks and drifted across the floor to form dunes under furniture. Mikhail followed her into her kitchen, cramped enough to excuse his standing close behind her. Funny that though their bodies communed in the tango, they had to begin the dance all over again now. She set the electric kettle to boil water for tea and uncovered a plate of brownies. Mikhail didn't want tea.

"Do you have any vodka?"

"I don't drink."

"Your religion?"

"I just don't."

"Part of my Russian heritage, drinking too much vodka and not believing in God."

"I think a lot of Russians believe in God."

"Not as many as drink too much vodka."

"There's a beer someone left here."

"Someone. Didn't last to finish his six-pack?"

"It wasn't like that."

She sat beside him on the yellow sofa. It was short, more of a loveseat, which was fine with Mikhail. The brownies weren't what he would choose to go with beer, but they were chewy and gave him a nice sugar rush. Juniper ate hers in big, appreciative bites. When she'd finished she scavenged crumbs that had scattered inside the collar of her blouse. Mikhail caught her hands. "You're a sloppy eater." He undid her top two buttons. "I think another fell in here."

"You're rushing things a bit."

"Who knows how much time anyone has left? It's a shame to waste it on subtleties when we both know what we want."

Juniper licked a crumb from his finger. "Waste not, want not, my mother always said."

Mikhail lifted Juniper's hair and kissed her neck. The kettle made a ruckus and clicked off. Juniper ignored it. She helped Mikhail with buttons and hooks and zips. He suspected she was disappointed with what she found when they were mostly naked, but he knew how to deal with that. "Juniper, Juniper, there's plenty of you for both of us, and see how I stand in awe."

"I'm actually Portland, Portland Juniper Berlin. I feel like an atlas if I use my whole name."

"An atlas, fine. I, the brave explorer Mikhail Petrovich Kuzmin, trace the route between landmarks." Mikhail touched one breast and ran his finger down it, over the rise of her belly into her pubic jungle, around and up again to the other. He sang to her in a baritone more breath than voice:

> *I see the map*
> *and I recall that not so*
> *long ago*
> *I used to live beside a waterfall*
> *that made the pussy*
> *willows damp*
> *in the spring.*

She swelled before him like a landscape, smooth expanses and hidden caves—even more like his grandmother's nesting matryoshka doll. He was holding a good-sized rounded hunk of mature womanhood, but he felt her younger, too, as if he could take her apart in the middle and find the dewy labia of her eighteen-year-old self. She mumbled against his lips. "Did you make up that song?"

"I dreamed it."

"Is that true?"

"Maybe. We're here, and where's Argentina? Ah, in the southern hemisphere, at the bottom of the world. We must explore it!"

"Are you going to Argentina?"

"Right now, yes."

Chapter Eleven

~~Howard's~~ End

Rosalie fell silent at the end of her tale about her husband's dying. Firelight sparkled in her wine glass, and in a tear overflowing onto her cheek. Dan wiped away her tear with one knuckle. He detested death stories. They provoked memories and hallucinations that made his toes curl and ice crystallize in his heart. Touching Rosalie's warm cheek helped quell this ghoulishness. Another tear swelled and trembled on her lower lid; this time he would cup her cheek in his palm, and if she didn't flinch, kiss it away. Something nudged Dan's ankle. He looked down into Roger the Dog's red-rimmed eyes. Roger's toothy underbite gripped an animal knee bone fresh from the butcher, raw flesh clinging around the joint. Roger dropped the bone on Dan's foot and looked to Rosalie for her approval.

She dabbed the tear from her eye. "He likes you!"

Dan felt the dead meat through his sock, gelid and clammy. Bile rose in his throat. His ears filled with the high-pitched clangor that always presaged his panic attacks. He watched himself set his wine glass on the coffee table in jerky, strobing increments. If he let the death thoughts get him, Rosalie would see him helpless, on hands and knees. He had to escape while he could stand. He was barely aware of Rosalie giving him his jacket and a puzzled look. Outside, he trotted toward town until he was hot and out of breath, which didn't take long. His gasps proved he remained among the living.

Rosalie finished her wine by the fire. She finished Dan's, too, while Roger gnawed and slavered over his lamb bone on the hearth. Dan was a strange one, but whole and healthy. She'd learned to appreciate that. You had to be alert with older men, and men near her age were all in that category now. Howard had been a good deal older than she was, but she'd been too young to grasp the implications when they met. If she'd been in love with him, she couldn't remember it. She'd made a deal with the devil and had no right to complain.

She'd adapted to the petty humiliations, never sure which of the women they mingled with socially also mingled with her husband in more intimate settings, which hands she shook had also stroked her husband's naked parts. It was more awkward for Howard's paramours, each surmising she was his only one, than for her. He always came home. The last few years with Howard had been their best, as he aged and grew more enthralled with conquering mountains than climbing into taboo beds. With the stepchildren reared, and Rosalie busy with her work, she didn't mind that Howard slipped off now and then.

Sometimes he went only as far as the room in their Manhattan apartment where he kept his trains. His model-railroad obsession had struck her as bizarrely against type—the adorable miniature towns populated by wee people. Watching him hunkered amid his models, she understood it better. They were like a continuum of the city that spread below their floor-to-ceiling windows, but their every move was dependent upon Howard's omnipotent rule.

Other times, he disappeared for days with no plausible explanation. If she'd known, could she have stopped his gambling as the stakes skyrocketed, as he siphoned all he could from their assets and mined her business accounts—play-money skimmed off the top, as he saw it? He dug himself into a hole undetectable except to those he'd lost to. Scenting impending shortage, they began calling in his debts.

Howard hadn't displayed his habitual ebullience on Kilimanjaro. They'd both had altitude sickness at the summit. Rosalie wrote it off to bad water. How long could Howard have buttressed his whole tottering financial structure if his health hadn't imploded first? After his death, it fell upon Rosalie to dig out from the rubble. Other things died with him—for one, her understanding of her place in the world. Virtually everything she thought she owned belonged to someone else, including her interior design business. Her stepchildren's loyalties belonged to their mother, and any vestigial affection they bore Rosalie evaporated with their vanishing inheritance. The generous insurance benefit Howard bequeathed her wasn't so generous after she'd settled out of court with his kids and paid her lawyers, some of whom also had gambling debts to collect. The hardest part, though, had been killing Howard.

Howard had dominated Rosalie through his formidable personality; she had no tenderness to draw from when he lay helpless to exert his will. Howard would have died anyway. How long would it have been? Years more maybe, years wiping his drool and worse, years of his pathetic gratitude for her ministrations, caring for him the way she would have cared for the baby he'd denied her. Howard would loathe it, Rosalie told herself, he would rather die. She told herself that after the fact. At the time, she acted, or failed to act (a fine distinction) without allowing herself to think, watching Howard's death unfold with awful fascination, as though it were only one of many possible consequences, as though she could replay the scene with some other outcome if this one wasn't to their liking, one where she'd given him his medication when he needed it, one where she'd called for help.

It could have happened the way she said it did. They'd had a quiet Sunday. The housekeeper and dog-walker had come and gone. Rosalie read the *Times* aloud, played Howard's Beethoven quartets at the resounding decibels he preferred, fed him what little he would eat. She *might* have been sleeping when Howard rang for her. If the weekend nurse's teenage daughter hadn't been in an accident that Saturday, perhaps Howard would still be alive. Rosalie shuddered at the thought.

She'd met Howard's eyes as she stood beside his bed and did nothing. Had his answering glare been fear or complicity? She couldn't make out the meaning behind the sounds gurgling in his throat. Whether his tears were from emotion or just uncontrolled leaking secretions was impossible to tell; she'd never seen Howard cry. Soon, it all stopped. She kissed goodbye the poor slack face she'd shaved tenderly that morning. She tucked the comforter around his shoulders and lay beside him until he cooled, before she went to bed in her own room and thrashed sleepless until daylight.

After Howard's body was removed, Rosalie sat for a while with his trains. The huge windows were triple-glazed, the silence in the apartment accusing. Blue shadows sped across the panorama outside. Sun glinting on the other high-rises made the city look alive. Rosalie wasn't fooled: everyone there was racing toward death, just as Howard had been. Dust had accumulated on the Lilliputian city inside, on its minuscule trees and people. One hapless neighborhood was in disarray from Howard's fall against it. Rosalie found a driverless toy ambulance and moved it where the need seemed greatest for a first responder. A blond figure like herself leaned half off a balcony, one arm raised in a plea for help, or in triumph at her survival.

The medicinal smell of Howard's dying breath disturbed Rosalie's sleep even now, though she'd moved as far as she could from anyone and anything they'd known together. She'd done her best to conserve fond memories of Howard, even some she suspected she'd made up, sealed in the back of her mind, where they would never diminish, and never intrude. Rosalie strove for clean and perfect independence in her environment, her body, her mind—a happy new life, not a happy ending, not yet. She loved the clear mountain air and snowmelt water that gushed from the Cascades. She loved her house, every object, every finish, every lamp, cup, cushion, and chair chosen to suit herself, nothing casually accumulated, no antiques, everything new and impeccable. She'd eradicated everything left over from her old life, except Roger the Dog. She loved him, of course she did. He gave her his unstinting trueheartedness, an allegiance he'd transferred to her after Howard's death. And yet, he was sole witness to his master's final weekend. Sometimes his head lay in her lap heavy with the past. It was wrong to harbor mixed feelings about a dog.

Chapter Twelve

River

Juniper hadn't looked ahead to what would happen after that first dalliance (the word seemed to fit the situation) with Mikhail. They'd forgotten to exchange phone numbers in the drowsy afterglow. She'd lounged naked on the yellow sofa and nibbled brownies, admiring his wide shoulders as he dressed. He was out of shape, but the material was there if he put in gym time. His hands and feet were small for his body, too, more delicate and shapely than hers, but he used it all to such good effect that what might be considered drawbacks became titillating in her eyes. He'd pulled her up to kiss goodbye, and run those hands down her body again. *Get some vodka for next time.* She'd laughed. That was the closest to any promises they'd made between them.

Nor had Mikhail shown up at her door again that week, at least not while she was home. The caterer she worked for had scheduled three wedding receptions, a bat mitzvah, and someone's hundredth birthday party. Juniper cooked and prepped, served and tended bar every day and late into most nights. Tuesday was her regular day off. Through breakfast and laundry, she thought about giving River a birthday call.

River was a spring baby, born two weeks early, roaring strong, earning his name. Greg's mother dredged up the memory of a red-haired aunt and there was much discussion about recessive genes' unpredictable persistence. What astounded everyone was River's precocious musicality. By four he picked out chords on the guitar Greg had long given up on. Greg declared himself a full-time dad in his off seasons, devoting himself to River's music lessons and recitals and competitions. Juniper waited tables and served cocktails in high-end restaurants year round, often with two jobs at a time, as her own diffuse aspirations drifted, replaced by ambition for her son. River was never interested in following Greg into the wilderness. If he'd been along on the trip where Greg met Glory, perhaps the family narrative would have changed. Greg was alone and Glory was, too, and all that followed was, if not inevitable, not surprising to Juniper.

Dakota haunted her dreams, and as his features surfaced more and more through River's face, he haunted her waking hours, too. When River reached adolescence, Dakota walked again, identical in his lanky frame, with the difference that River was filled with love for Juniper. He loved Greg, too, and that love spilled over into love for Glory when she came along. His loyalties stretched, the effort to be a good son to everybody took its toll. At sixteen, River began to drink, and by eighteen the binges had begun to blur. His fingers became less agile on the guitar strings, he showed up unreliably for gigs. His guaranteed music scholarship vaporized. Glory's influence got him a job with a casino band, and he moved to Las Vegas to live with her and Greg.

For Juniper his leaving was a double loss, her culpability in Dakota's fall come home to roost. She hadn't been in love with Dakota, but loving River without reservation meant loving what she saw of Dakota through him, praying the real Dakota was alive and well, but never to reappear. Anyone who saw the father would recognize him in the son, and the truth of River's conception would cause heartbreak all around. When River moved out, Dakota became the invisible man who shadowed Juniper everywhere. How far could a shadow stretch? His had followed her to this town with the bright high desert spreading to the east of its river and the mountains rising to the west. The only vindication for her adultery with Dakota was the son they'd produced.

She missed her boy beyond anything she could have imagined before she was a mother, no matter he was grown up. She never knew for sure when

River might be asleep or working; night and day were different in Las Vegas than in Juniper's world. She sent him a happy birthday text with a smiley emoticon and a string of twinkly hearts, and opened her closet to dress for tango.

Chapter Thirteen

Lesson Six: Argentine Dreams

Esteban's core six persisted, whether for love of the dance, or their Argentine dreams, or because they'd paid for eight lessons and wanted to get their money's worth. Esteban had emailed Aurelia again, promising they were all on board and he'd send the deposit soon. Though she said nothing about his video, her reply was marginally warmer. Aurelia wouldn't be impressed if he brought her shambling, undisciplined absolute beginners. He had to groom them, pull back, devote more time to the basics at the risk of losing them through boredom.

They didn't seem bored this evening. Esteban saw more energy in their warm-up walk. He credited his teaching the *cabeceo* the last time, forcing them out of their shells. Older students like these were always self-conscious, repressed, he suspected, sexually deprived, if in fact they were interested in sex. That was a crazy thought. Some weren't that much older than he was, and his interest certainly hadn't dwindled. He was saving himself for Aurelia. Look at the renowned *milongueros*—old men dancing with women in their thirties, even, and the women's faces blissful. He'd seen women in their eighties dancing so beautifully that young men were thrilled to lead them. Sometimes tango was better than sex.

Dan had used the week to examine all the ways he was inadequate to the task of behaving like a healthy human being. Ghosts made a morbid scrim between him and those he would reach out to. He'd asked little of himself with Rosalie, a normal conversation by the fire, not a real date. What counted as a date these days? Never mind, he'd failed. He replayed the evening over and over, a movie with a plot that went nowhere. He'd dreaded facing her at tango class, that she would laugh at him or ignore him, counting him out of her life. None of that happened. She was walking in the circle when he arrived, and she gave him a tiny wave, not raising her hand above her waist.

Esteban called to the women in the circle to walk backwards, lengthen their legs, collect their feet between steps. Mikhail had been walking behind Juniper, now he faced her as they walked. Her breasts quivered with her steps. He could tell she was deliberately avoiding meeting his eyes, glancing over her shoulder, pretending concern about bumping into Dan, whose stride was shorter than hers. He was sure she wasn't embarrassed about their amorous interlude. Most likely she was teasing him, trying to seduce him into pursuing her. Well, he was clever at games, and two could play at that one.

Esteban could see they were all beginning to feel more confident about themselves—half the battle for him. He put on an easy Canaro piece and set them walking in close embrace with partners while he watched and called out corrections, more *apilado* to make space for the feet, chests together, tailbone tucked in, shoulders relaxed, sternum lifted. *Breathe! Everyone up, up, up, no shrinking! Leads, stand proud, your role is to make your follow look good!*

Rosalie liked that concept; she'd take any boost she could get. She'd done something wrong with Mikhail and Dan, something clumsy that had discouraged them both. She didn't see either man as life-mate material, but someone out there must be, and she wanted to be ready when they met. Mikhail and Dan offered practice for reentering the world without Howard. He'd been a fortress to her, prison and protection. Life with him had been a forced march through luxury. She felt like an ex-con emerging into dubious freedom, released from a forty-year sentence. She stood taller on the balls of her feet.

ESTEBAN WORKED THEM UNTIL THEY WERE DIZZY. "Bravo! I can see you all with me in Argentina. Let me tell you a story." He made a supple *sacada* step to the side. "One summer evening in Buenos Aires, I can't see out through the rain on my windows. My last night in the Paris of South America, I have to tango no matter what. I take an umbrella and wade through the streets to the milonga at *Lo de Celia*. I'm half expecting the place to be empty, but as I climb the stairs, I hear the music. The floor's packed with dancers. Nothing stops them. They're still going when I leave at three a.m."

He blinked, as though returning reluctantly. "Then there's the Sunderland Club, and the upstairs ballroom at the *Confitería Ideal*, and *El Beso*. Romance and tango everywhere, in San Telmo especially, couples dancing in the streets. Wait till you see what the women do in stiletto heels on cobblestones!"

Esteban wound himself up with his own zeal, improvising on scenes he'd harvested from videos, building to his grand finale: "In two weeks, for our eighth lesson, I'm hosting an authentic milonga, a social dance, right here, a reward for your marvelous progress in class. A taste of Argentina! For next week, ladies bring heels to practice in, gentlemen, light shoes with smooth soles."

He clapped his hands, and his six applauded him in return. He'd fed their fantasies. They looked pleased as trained seals thrown a fish. No, he didn't mean that, Esteban chided himself. These people were key to his future happiness. He would make up for his bad thoughts and find his final three with his mini-milonga. Tango lovers were like cockroaches—they were countless, but they hid in the woodwork until the conditions were right.

Something had poisoned whatever tango community existed in this small town, and they were all in hiding, not unusual among people passionate about the dance. None had sent out feelers when he advertised his beginner class, but they might for a milonga. Somehow he would recruit a group for Aurelia. To improve his chances his students had to look appealing as partners, or no experienced dancer would come further than the door. Especially his leads. There were never enough of them to satisfy the women.

Chapter Fourteen

Body Memory

The more Esteban talked, the more his Buenos Aires sounded different from the city Dan had known; his attention drifted as Esteban blathered on and on. Dan hadn't tangoed the several months he'd lived in Argentina nearly thirty years before. He'd written off the dancing he'd seen in the streets as tourist bait. His work there had been complicated by the peculiar, to his ear, Spanish spoken by the *Porteños*—most of whom had at least one Italian grandmother—and by involvement with a woman. The affair had taken place in a darkened room at odd hours, lubricated by local wine and poor judgment. Something about the woman, her smell, her voice's timbre, reminded him of his dead wife. He'd risked ruin on many levels because with her he'd been able to imagine himself touching Naomi. This was the dangerous part, the memory no-go zone Esteban's bloviating led him into, where he was helpless to resist. Dan left class with the avalanche of recollection already threatening to crush him.

When Dan thought of his wife he saw her eyes first, translucent green. *Like a tropical sea on a sunny day,* someone had described them. He could never find the words; that had been his problem. He spent so much time looking for the right words for his plans and concerns that once he had them lined up, like soldiers ready to march, Naomi would've already gone ahead into territory that felt precarious to him. But sometimes he could be reckless, too—it had been Dan's childhood fantasy that lured them out West. Who bases a major life decision on old movies? He had. In every Western he'd watched as a kid, it wasn't the blazing action of the heroes and villains that grabbed him, it was sun-washed distances, riders flickering through mirages on the desert, wide silence that echoed horses' clopping hooves.

Compared to that, every corner of their neighborhood in Manhattan seemed a dead end, every park a futile effort to recollect nature. Two babies in four years had frayed Naomi's identity. Her career had fizzled in ways she hadn't foreseen when her biological clock had been ticking to its inexorable end times. Younger, and childless, barracudas had swarmed in behind her. Dan persuaded her to buy into his scheme.

They hopscotched across flyover country, visiting her aunt in Ohio, his cousin in Minneapolis. Nothing flat appealed. Their spirits soared when they saw their first real mountains, but they kept in mind the practicalities: Wyoming was too isolated, Idaho too conservative. Portland seemed just right—enough city to find work, glacial peaks on the skyline, the high desert over the Cascades to the east, and the ocean to the west. They settled in, like Goldilocks.

Naomi delighted in the lilacs and roses and lilies that bloomed around their rented bungalow that spring. She filled vases she bought at the Saturday market for every room. She made new friends among the moms volunteering at their sons' preschool and kindergarten, and joined a book group, something she'd sworn never to do. Dan found a dull bureaucratic job with a Federal agency. He could bus across the Willamette from his office and be home in time to fix dinner. He anchored their lives around the dinner table, one certain point in their days. He cooked, Naomi and the boys obeyed when he called, the younger son proudly graduated from his highchair, eating with a spoon.

In his anguished imagination now, Dan saw his sons as they would have been: sibling spats and reconciliations over toys and attention. Later, surly teenagers breaking his rules. He saw his wife's eyes looking into his, reassuring him when he worried about their driving or schoolwork, or God forbid, drugs.

Every weekend that summer they explored. They found the coastal scenery spectacular, the Pacific colder and deeper and with bigger waves than the Atlantic. They tried to explain Mount St. Helens to the boys, its volcanic magnitude greater than they could take in themselves. They were all astonished to be able to play in snow on Mount Hood on the Fourth of July. Everything was larger and cleaner and fresher than the lives they'd lived until then. They grew braver, more confident they belonged. Dan bought hiking guidebooks, and they traded in their Audi sedan for a used four-by-four to handle old logging roads to more-remote trailheads. He and Naomi felt drunk with adventure.

They didn't yet understand the seasons in their adopted home, not the way people do with body memory over time. They'd been warned weather could change quickly in the mountains. They'd seen afternoon rainstorms sweep in from sky that was clear in the mornings. They always carried waterproof gear, even on short hikes, and laughed that they hadn't melted yet. The long summer segued into autumn, golden with aspen, red with sumac and maple, aglow in low-angled sun that seemed endless. Dan and Naomi talked about buying skis for themselves and the boys.

The Saturday before Halloween dawned sunny and dry, demanding one last hike. They'd read about a deserted fire lookout up a long road with a short trail to the top and a view over everything. Dan would tote the younger boy in his carrier on his back up the hard part. Their older son had taken to hiking like a baby mountain goat and, though his legs were short, he had an iron will and a child's profligate energy.

They left the city early, driving east into the sun. Other people had the same idea, the parking pullouts at trailheads along the highway jammed with cars. Dan was smug about the route they'd chosen, which took them off the pavement onto a numbered forest road. Even as it climbed and grew rough it was nothing their sturdy four-by-four couldn't handle. The boys whooped and cheered as he steered through the deepening ruts with the car tilting and righting itself. Dan followed the guidebook's directions precisely, watching the odometer, finding the branch road exactly where it was described, two-point-seven miles up, and another six-tenths on, to the tight turnaround, which was blessedly empty. He turned the car right away, in case someone else came along. He didn't want to test his ability to reverse down the way they'd come, though he figured he could do it if he had to. The evergreen forest was colder than they'd expected at over four thousand feet. Naomi unpacked their extra fleece jackets and made the boys wear the hand-knit hats that were another Saturday market find. They complained the hats scratched. Naomi took the pack with sandwiches and cookies and water. The younger boy fretted when they lifted him into the carrier, then snuggled against Dan's back.

His brother galloped ahead.

They had the trail to themselves. It could have been any century once the car disappeared among the evergreens. A jay's cry and a vee of Canada geese honking above the treetops disturbed the quiet. The guidebook was right about the trail's steepness, too. They were heartened to break through the tree line, but they'd expected to come out into sunshine. While they'd been in the woods, clouds had surged over the mountains from the north and east. The usual pattern had been for weather to flow over the Coast Range from the west. Nevertheless, it was their last hike of the year, and they weren't quitters. The older boy was forging up the rocky half mile to the lookout. Dan's back was feeling the younger boy's weight. He wouldn't be getting carried next year, but being dad meant being stronger than anything in his sons' eyes.

The picnic on the summit was an anticlimax, nothing left of the fire lookout but a foundation and broken glass. Clouds had closed in until the only real view was themselves on the barren outcrop. Later, Dan wished he'd looked more at the others rather than concentrating on the sandwich Naomi passed him. He didn't like to admit how much carrying their little boy had taken out of him. He was bordering on forty and for the first time felt his age. Naomi urged them to eat quickly.

Before they'd gotten to the cookies, snow arrived, no warning flakes, seemingly from nowhere and from everywhere, if not a blizzard, something very like one. They followed their instincts, ducking beneath an overhanging boulder. The boys cheered, they weren't frightened yet. As the world turned white, Dan tried to remember where they'd left the trail. They couldn't afford to wait for the storm to stop, because it might not. He kept his voice calm, telling the others they had to start down. They put on their rain ponchos for another warm layer. Despite the ache in his back, Dan was glad to have his son's body heat combining with his own, the little arms wrapping his neck. They retraced their path as best they could, orienting to the lookout ruins, and Dan led them off the summit with more confidence than he felt.

He was sure they were on the trail. Naomi pointed out familiar-looking rock configurations, irritating him with the implication that he might not be certain. Everything looked different going the opposite direction and increasingly hidden under snow. He kept his relief to himself when they came to the woods and found the trail visible in places where the snow lay thinner beneath the trees. Naomi brushed snow off the older boy's poncho hood. The little one had pushed his hood back, pulled off his scratchy hat and tossed it somewhere. His ears were red with cold. He had tears in his eyes, whether from pain or fear of the scolding he knew he'd get for his rebellion. Naomi wrapped his head in her scarf and pulled her own collar tighter without taking time for reproaches. The older boy, stoic, excited at their adventure so far, complained his toes and fingers were numb. They hurried on through the woods, losing the trail, always finding it again, and finally coming out into the clearing where their car waited like a humped white beast.

It started easily despite the cold. Naomi and the boys held their hands to the heat vents inside as the car warmed, while Dan brushed snow off the windows. More was falling fast, accumulating even as he cleared it. He got in and set the wipers on high. He could see the road, or at least the gap in the trees where the road cut through. He released the brake, proud of his foresight in turning the car when they arrived. The boys were crying now over their painfully thawing hands. Naomi comforted them with the last cookies.

Dan leaned closer to the windshield and switched on the fog lights. They made the white curtain outside even more opaque. The spiraling snow distorted what little he could see, wraithlike tree shapes looming ahead where he didn't think they should be. He drove slowly, trying not to let Naomi notice his tentativeness, feeling his way as much as seeing it. The little one squirmed to see out and released his booster-seat buckle. Naomi leaned over her seat to refasten the belt. The car jolted into an invisible rut. Dan wrenched the wheel to correct for it. The car listed further to the right with a grinding sound before he could stop. They sat at an angle, Dan on the high side. He got out cautiously, to not disturb the balance. He'd misjudged the road by a few crucial inches and the right front tire had slid off the edge. How deep the drop it hung over was, he could only judge by his memory of that long ago season, the morning.

Up till then he'd felt more or less in control, doing the right things with the expected results. Now, no matter how hard he pushed as Naomi accelerated in reverse, no matter how she worked the gears, the three other wheels couldn't pull the fourth back onto the road. They'd high-centered on a rock or a log. The boys watched with interest, and with infinite trust. Dan had one last option. They were hardly more than three miles from the highway, all downhill. He could hike it in an hour, less if he took shortcuts across the curves, and hail a ride to get help. The boys were too small to make the walk. They'd wait with Naomi. Dan got into the car and explained his plan. He kissed them all goodbye. Naomi made him put on the remaining knit hat before she let him go. It was tight on his head, and the boys were right, it did scratch. She wiped condensation off the inside of the window, her eyes wide and worried through it as she waved goodbye, and Dan set off.

He imagined Naomi reassured by his stride

through the powder. When he looked back to wave again the car was invisible in the swirling white. He stayed on the road, watching for a chance to cut through the woods directly, until he spotted a slope that seemed easy to follow straight to the next switchback. He slid down it, clutching low branches for balance. A sharp one gashed his palm. He didn't notice until the blood made his grip slippery. It took longer than he'd expected to come out on the road again, and he decided to stay on it rather than risk some other injury that might slow him.

Snow melted in his shoes. They were lightweight, designed to keep his feet cool. His wet socks bunched and began to rub a blister on his heel that stung even though he couldn't feel his toes. He walked, hands deep in his pockets, head bent, snow spinning at his face and into his eyes when he looked up to check the road. It was wider than he remembered, and had fewer curves. Places always seemed different when you'd seen them before than when it was your first time there. He pictured Naomi and the boys warm in the car, and was thankful he'd filled the gas tank on their way to the mountains. An annoying melody, something he'd heard in a supermarket, played through his head to the rhythm of his steps. He couldn't recall the words. He walked on. That was all he could do, just keep walking.

Chapter Fifteen

Tango Shoes

Neither Dan nor Mikhail were to be seen when Juniper left the Norwegian hall with Rosalie. They'd been talking about tango shoes, a penchant the two women shared. Rosalie's Lexus was the only car in the parking lot besides Esteban's Corolla. Juniper would have accepted Rosalie's offer of a ride if it hadn't been another spring-like evening. On her way home, she stood for a while in the middle of the footbridge, watching the moon's rippling reflection, letting her thoughts flow with its mystery. She was in no hurry to return to an empty house.

Mikhail was waiting, leaning against her door. "You took your time. I thought you'd gone home with someone else."

"Likely."

He didn't explain why he hadn't called and she didn't ask why he was there. He followed her inside, one hand cupping her bottom. "I brought you a present, something to eat after tango."

"Nothing with crumbs."

"No crumbs, not a one. Chocolates. Isn't that what a man's supposed to bring?"

"Sweet, old-fashioned, aren't you?" Juniper bit the top off a chocolate. She made sure Mikhail saw her tongue wrap around the cream filling before she crushed the rest between her teeth.

Mikhail held out the box to her. "Take another."

"For goodness sake, let me get my coat off. I have something for you, too." In the kitchen, Juniper's cats materialized and rubbed against her ankles. She pulled a bottle from the freezer. "Look here."

"Vodka!"

"Courtesy a nice young man who conked out before he could finish it at his wedding party. I promise you, they'll never miss it."

Mikhail poured vodka into a juice glass and watched while Juniper took off her coat. "Don't be shy, take off more. Pretend I'm not here."

"Why would I take off more if you weren't here? Does chocolate go with vodka?"

"Let's find out."

Their tongues competed for a chocolate cream in Juniper's mouth until Juniper laughed. "Wait, I want you to hear what I downloaded."

Tango music filled the room. Mikhail saluted her with his drink *to the beautiful lady* then tossed it back in one gulp and set his glass on the table. "Dance with me."

They danced a short circle, shoving aside furniture and piles of books with their feet. Juniper's yellow cat watched from under the table, the other turned tail out the cat door.

"Esteban says your job as lead is to make me look good."

Mikhail smirked. "Take off your clothes, then."

"I look better dressed."

"Your opinion. Am I not the lead? Your job is to follow."

With each circuit of the room Juniper discarded another layer until she danced naked in bare feet. "Now you."

While Mikhail undressed, Juniper rummaged in her closet and came up with a pair of red stilettos. Mikhail grinned as she fastened the straps. "I'd better be a good lead then. It'll be painful if you step on me now with those."

"Pleasure and pain are never far apart. Give us another chocolate."

Chapter Sixteen

Staying Alive

Dan tramped past microbrew pubs and food carts in his neighborhood, oblivious to the Mexican, Indian, Asian-Fusion aromas that usually made him salivate on his way home. He bumped shoulders with other pedestrians, a bicyclist swerved around him, and a car honked at an intersection—Dan was still lost in those snowy woods.

Several times he thought he saw someone ahead and called out. The man (he was sure it was a man, though it might have been a deer) didn't turn. The snow, up to his knees, muffled all sounds. He plowed through it. The man disappeared around a bend, and when Dan got there his footprints had filled in, which was odd, since the snow was slowing, the flakes larger and lazier as though they, too, were exhausted by the storm, until they stopped altogether. Everything lay in shadowless white. The snow underfoot grew wetter; it clumped on Dan's boots and made them heavy. When he checked his watch, the numbers didn't make sense. The road angled up. That shouldn't happen—they'd driven steadily up on their way in, all the way out had to be down.

Dan didn't like what he saw. These hills were laced with logging roads long unused for their original purpose. His shortcut had landed him on the wrong one. He should retrace his steps, or… he listened. He thought he heard cars on the highway. That would be right. He took off the knit hat covering his ears. Yes, a rushing sound downhill from where he stood. He abandoned the road. Close to his goal he could afford to take the chance. The terrain, softened by snow, looked smoother than it was. He clambered over hidden undergrowth, detoured around fallen trees, stopping to listen for the highway, adjusting his direction according to the sound growing louder. Something was not quite right about it; it wasn't exactly the sound of tires on pavement, but it was the only sound there was, and getting close.

When the ground gave way, Dan yelled and flung up his arms. He tumbled into a ravine and a fast-flowing stream that ran black and clear. Thin ice glazed its eddies, its roar disproportionate to its small size against the forest's otherwise utter silence. Dan climbed out on the other side, soaked to his thighs.

His mind and body felt detached from each other, and even from himself. He wanted to sleep but he couldn't think how to stop his body. It moved on reflexively downhill, always downhill. His clothes chafed, unbearable against his skin, impediments to the movement that was its own necessity. The hat was long gone. He tore off his jacket, then his shirt. It was his pants that were the most obstructive. To take them off he'd have to stop, and that was unbearable, too. His mind went dormant, no more messages incoming or sent than were needed to keep him upright. At some point his feet found another road.

Dan climbed the stairs to his apartment. He sagged onto his futon and punished himself by remembering everything, even the parts he hadn't seen. The hunters who found him called the forest rangers, who wouldn't let him go back up with the search-and-rescue team. The only heroism they allowed him was to form the name of the lookout trail and the three precious names of his family, words that had waited for that moment, held on his tongue after all others were lost to the cold. When he tried to tear off the blankets, rip out the IV needles, fight his way out of the ambulance, EMTs sedated him. He could never sort out later whether it would have been worse, if worse was even possible, to be with the rescuers when they found the car, as motionless beneath the white as anything else on that mountain that day. To have scraped snow off the windshield and seen Naomi with the boys cuddled in her lap in the back seat, the little one with his thumb frozen in his mouth, the older boy's blue fingers coiled in his mother's hair, her cheek resting on his head. Their eyes would have been closed; that was a mercy. He'd killed them as sure as the storm had, his heedless charge to be their hero the wrong choice, when his greatest heroic act would have been to first clear the tailpipe jammed into the embankment. Their picture was so vivid he believed he'd been there with them. For a very long time he wished he had been, to fall asleep together forever.

HE STAYED ALIVE TO PRESERVE THEIR MEMORY, making the whole cottage their temple, then—when he couldn't bear to sequester himself with his guilt any longer—carrying a more portable altar in his mind. Surviving became a necessary burden he accepted to prove his strength to Naomi. He'd always reckoned her the strong one, and he continued to lean on her in ways he understood weren't sensible or sane. Dan knew she would hate their conversations in bed, in the dark where he couldn't see her absence. She would hate that the things she said from her empty pillow became increasingly his, ascribed to her, that when she disagreed with his opinions it was his usual internal debate, his endless effort to make the right choice.

A few weeks after he'd returned to work Dan was summoned upstairs. In an office with a Mt. Hood view he met a man in a suit more carefully tailored than the conventional bureaucrat's. His life changed again with their handshake. The government being the government, Dan had to do some training courses to justify the higher pay grade before he could take on his new job. He'd never handled a gun, and had never intended to. The adrenaline surge he got from target practice surprised him. It felt good to do something completely different from his old self, something Naomi wouldn't come near, alive or dead, or let their boys know about, either. Dan understood it was more than his loyalty and diligence that attracted his new boss; it was that he was tied to no one, with nothing to lose, the lone cowboy ready to ride.

Who better for undercover intelligence work than an apparent nonentity of no clear ethnic origin? Change his clothes and posture, his way of speaking and using his eyes, and Dan could slot in anywhere along the Asian-European spectrum, with stops along the way for Indian (Eastern or Western) and Latino. People didn't look at one another too deeply after the first impression. That was how he'd ended up on assignment in Argentina.

Part of his difficulty with retirement lay in plowing back through those professional identities to find his own, whatever that meant. He felt like a serial killer, ruthlessly offing those other selves until the last man standing had to be him. Dan found himself monochrome and meaningless, as though he'd killed his real personality and been left with this irrelevant shell. Of course he didn't impress Rosalie. How likely was it she would believe his true story if he told her—any of his stories? Dan's alternate personalities had served as companions, buffering his howling internal vacancy. Once they were gone, he found he had to face the void. He'd moved back as close as he could bear to where the worst thing possible had happened. What had he hoped, to feel near his lost family, to fix the unfixable? Seeking the not-sure-what, he'd thus far failed to find peace.

Chapter Seventeen

Lesson Seven: Connection

THE MEN WERE MORE HEAVY-FOOTED THAN USUAL, wearing their variations on the smooth-soled dance shoe theme—none like Esteban's light Italian numbers, though Dan's came close. The white-haired woman wobbled in low heels; Rosalie seemed blasé in stilettos. Juniper showed off three-inch leopard print *Comme il Fauts* she'd snared on eBay. *Genuine tango shoes from Argentina*, she was quick to point out. Dancing in socks had lent a playful air to their tango classes; they clearly felt more serious in shoes. Esteban was amused at their solemnity, like large toddlers. They had no idea how far they had to go, imagining themselves becoming proficient.

His antennae were up for the dynamics among them. Competition was stimulating if it didn't grow into outright hostility. Nothing was more destructive to a tango group than love triangles—the atmosphere should comprise more abstract romance, the potential hovering, but non-specific, sexuality in the air, not on the ground. Mikhail and Rosalie were ignoring each other. That could be tricky. Juniper seemed fine with everybody, the other two women exclaiming over her shoes. It wasn't unusual for men to be a little stand-offish with each other until they could bond via football or something else that showcased their masculinity. He got them all walking to warm up. The best strategy was to keep everybody moving and give them something to think about. *Tango is one step, then one step, your weight always on one foot at a time.*

Now they were trying *too* hard, lacking in joy. Their steps could be right, but they would look wrong, plodding. They needed inspiration. He would give them Aurelia. He should have done it weeks ago to win them over the way he'd been won. How had he expected to get his students to Buenos Aires without her help? He turned off the music, had them draw up folding chairs, and held his laptop open toward them. He cradled it in his arms, sharing Aurelia but asserting his possession.

Dan hid his flooding emotions. The video had to be at least ten years old, probably more. No matter how well "Aurelia" had aged, she would be closer to fifty now than the perhaps mid-thirties that the sylphlike dancer on the screen appeared to be. Twenty years younger than he was, at any rate. He would have recognized her anywhere. He'd known her as Beatriz, his illicit and insatiable paramour, their liaison in Buenos Aires spiced by menace.

He was still a novice at intelligence work when they met that long-ago Sunday afternoon. He'd been tracking a man named Raoul to what Dan's handlers hoped would be a conspirators' conclave. The hunt took him into the San Telmo market's cobblestone streets and wall-to-wall crowds. No problem, his cover identity as his boss's personal chef often led him through markets. If Dan was doing his usual best at nondescriptness, Raoul didn't know he was being tailed. Locals and foreigners jostled around stalls that sold the sad saga of Argentina's economic crisis during that decade. Anything was for sale that could be reasonably, or not so reasonably, of interest to anyone with money—old china and silver, figurines, paintings, leather work, clothing, jewelry, tango lessons. Stalking Raoul, Dan feigned interest in a food stall where beef from the pampas sizzled in its own fat. He was caught off guard when a sleek young woman, eyebrows arched over challenging dark eyes, threw her arms around his prey. She called to the man at the adjacent stall to mind hers, and darted away with Raoul in tow.

In the moment that Dan stood indecisive, the crowd closed around the couple. The woman's neighbor watched him with a quizzical smile. Dan's hands shook as he examined the drawings in her display—tango dancers captured with keen economy of line, each signed "Beatriz." He bought one and took it back to his room, where he hid it under the clothes in the suitcase he never fully unpacked. His impulse to hide the drawing told him all he needed to know about his motives: They were personal, and therefore forbidden by his job. He'd pledged to keep to his contract, but although Buenos Aires was full of stunning women, never before had he heard one speak in Naomi's voice.

He could justify his subsequent surveillance of Beatriz by her connection with Raoul. Dan returned to the market, bought another drawing, made conversation that bloomed effortlessly into flirtation. He congratulated himself on the suavity with which he seduced Beatriz, how soon they were meeting in her studio, one room with a French door to a balcony with two colorfully painted chairs and a potted rosemary plant. He never did understand whether or not she lived there, or if she had a home somewhere else. To be seen with her on the street would jeopardize his mission, and no telling what possessive violence Raoul would unleash. Beatriz told him she was afraid of her fiancé, too. She praised Dan's gentleness and watched the clock during their trysts. He had to be content with stolen hours. He'd wondered in later years if her voice really had been like Naomi's, if her scent he'd told himself brought Naomi back to him had resembled hers at all, or if, when he closed his eyes and imagined himself with his wife, it was what he needed to believe to reoccupy himself as a sexual being without feeling disloyal to the dead. His over-thinking came later rather than during the affair, when he could have used it.

In his work he was never shown the big picture. Too much knowledge was dangerous both to himself and to the security of each mission. What he did know was his agency was collaborating with others, gathering evidence against international weapons traffickers, one of whom was Raoul. What wasn't under Dan's official purview was the man's background in clandestine operations for Argentina's ferocious military junta a dozen years before. Raoul had specialized in throwing political enemies, bound and gagged, from helicopters far out over the ocean, and other less subtle means of maintaining control and extracting information. The legal ramifications of Raoul's past weren't the agency's business, a purely internal matter snarled in corruption at all levels, an issue Dan was glad to leave alone, except that Beatriz was engaged to marry this man he'd come to see as a monster.

Dan demonstrated his genius at espionage in the mad plot he hatched to rescue Beatriz from her fiancé and smuggle her out of the country. He wouldn't be the first operative to be lulled by pillow talk, but he was scrupulous about maintaining his fictional identity as a simple private chef. His bosses were getting testy about his failure to catch Raoul at anything more incriminating than carrying Beatriz off for overnights at his vineyard in the country. Dan would follow them at a distance, in a different car each time, and position himself to see if any visitors arrived. That none did infuriated him, and disclosed nothing. He redoubled his efforts, leaving Raoul unobserved only in the hours Dan stole to be with Beatriz. Raoul watched soccer, ate steak, and drank with a few male friends, none of whom had irreproachable pasts, but all deeply boring presents. So boring the agency announced the on-the-ground investigation was being axed; Dan and the agent posing as his putative businessman employer had eight hours to pack for a transfer to Bolivia.

It was time to activate his secret plan, first to reveal to Beatriz what he knew about Raoul's record, then to provide a way out. It was a busy Sunday and she refused to leave her market stall, so he took her aside and told her. He read her response to the news at first as distress, until she began to laugh—Naomi's laugh, but with a callous edge. "And you imagine I don't know those stories? Raoul is my brother's best friend since school. They served in the same army unit. Why you are telling me this?"

Beatriz's ridicule saved him from professional suicide. As he left the market he thought he glimpsed Raoul smirking over a gourd at a *maté* stall. Whether or not Beatriz shared her fiancé's fascist views and murderous tendencies, Dan had touched evil without recognizing it. He was the outsider who'd been duped by history's oldest trick. Whatever Raoul had been up to, it fit nicely into the hours Beatriz shared with Dan.

Dan wasn't surprised Beatriz had changed her name and taken up tango, one of Argentina's cottage industries, as a livelihood, nor that she had bewitched Esteban. Buenos Aires had a chaotic economy, and the tango community was a highly visible part of it. He'd long ago discovered that the six-degrees-of-separation rule was a joke. Wherever he'd worked in the world, two degrees was typical, three at a stretch. No way was Dan joining Esteban's tango tour.

"ARE YOU GOING TO ARGENTINA?" ROSALIE ASKED Mikhail when Esteban closed his laptop and set them dancing again. He asked her if she was, letting the implication hang that his answer might be contingent on hers. Neither answered the other's question. It wasn't a real question for him, though he'd been beguiled watching the tango *maestra*. Divorce lawyers' fees had chewed up his retirement savings. The new horizons he should be looking for related to employment, which at his age wasn't a happy prospect. Overseas travel wasn't in his immediate future, unless Rosalie.... No, it was too soon, and how did he know she hadn't blown her entire insurance payout on the Lexus? She might be all bait and switch. Mikhail put more panache into his steps, inspired by the man he'd seen leading in the video. With proper coaching, he told himself, he could look that good. He'd arrange for more lessons when Esteban came back from his tour.

Juniper was Mikhail's next partner. She whispered in his bad ear as they danced. It came through as sensation, words drowned by the music, but he caught the drift. He felt tired at the thought of dealing with Rosalie's intensity; he chose the bird in hand. For now he could hold Juniper in his arms and Rosalie in his mind, two birds with one stone. He laughed softly, wrapped his arm a little tighter around Juniper's back until his fingertips touched the side of her right breast.

Aurelia looked improbably familiar to Rosalie, too, though she didn't recognize the name. What was the occasion when they'd met? One of the many times she'd dined with Howard and another couple to occupy the wife while the two men talked unspecified business? She had an impression of the woman, charming and speaking heavily-accented English, but it was hardly a memory. Had they talked about tango? Was that how the idea got planted, lying dormant in Rosalie all those years because Howard hated to dance? She was falling in love with tango, but her interest in Esteban's tango tour flatlined with this connection to her past.

The door of the Norwegian's hall was like a fortune-teller's tool—depending on who left when, and with whom, entire stories could be woven, stories which might or might not prove true. Reading them took minimal intuition. Rosalie deemed herself fully qualified. Mikhail left so closely after Juniper this evening, while the others were still changing shoes, that not much prognostication was required. Rosalie allowed Dan a good look at her feet with their pearly nails from the morning's pedicure before she slipped on her flats.

DAN WATCHED ROSALIE'S HIGH ARCHES AND SOFT toes disappear into her shoes. Distracted by the desire to touch them, he groped for something to say. The disgusting dog was the first thing to pop up. "How's Roger?"

"Poor baby's worn out from the dog park. I left him snoring on my bed."

No chance of another dog walk. Dan hurtled ahead, one thought about beds prompting another. "My cat spends half his life sleeping on the bed, and hides under it the other half. He's afraid of everything—moths, spiders, even birds scare him."

"That's terrible, Dan. Poor thing! I have to meet him."

Dan was amazed at Rosalie's insistence, half-hoping it was a ruse to persuade him to take her home with him, as though he needed persuasion. She drove. He scarcely dared speak to her on the way in case he said something foolish and she changed her mind. Once there, Rosalie dropped her coat, went straight to the bedroom, and crouched on her knees on the floor. Dan envisioned a context where this would be a dream come true. She looked over her shoulder. "What's his name?"

"I call him Nobu."

Rosalie stuck her head under the bed. She murmured something, and Nobu responded with cat sounds for longer than a normal conversation between a human and a cat should last. Rosalie sat back and waited. "He has to think a bit."

Nobu emerged, an aged, bone-thin tabby, blinking enormous eyes in the light. He crawled into Rosalie's lap and began kneading, working up to a purr as she scratched beneath his chin. In the months since Dan had found the cat wandering in the street, he'd never come close. "How did you do that?"

Rosalie ignored the question. "His vision's failing and he can't hunt anymore. He's afraid you'll throw him out like his last people did and he'll starve. I told him you never would, that he'll always be warm and fed with you. He's a simple guy, that's all he needs to know."

"I named him after a cat we had when I was a

kid. *Nobu* means 'faith' in Japanese, but he's never got to trusting me."

"He doesn't speak Japanese. Do you?"

Dan sketched a slight bow. "Dan Shibata at your service. My father was from Japan."

Dan didn't generally talk about his father, and hardly anyone asked anymore. World War II receded into mythology as the survivors died; old soldiers barely able to stand held trembling flags at funerals. Everyone else had a surfeit of today's wars and terrors to preoccupy them. Dan had once met an immigrant businessman in Uruguay who'd been too young to fight in the European war years, but described with lifted chin and burning eyes returning the *Führer's* salute as he passed by train through his Austrian village *when the war was going well*. Dan had been more shocked than his profession permitted him to show—he'd never heard war stories from his Japanese father.

He hadn't known his father long, and was rarely admitted into his silence. His father, by sweeping a calligraphy brush over handmade paper, left marks that evinced more emotion than his scarred face. He painted indelible beauty to make up for his frozen mask, his students open-mouthed in awe when *awesome* was a word that held meaning. Dan's mother had been one of them. Spellbound by the master's art, she took on the role of intermediary between him and the American culture to which he never became reconciled. His new home with its foreign ways killed him as remorselessly as his war wounds, leaving few years to bequeath whatever life force remained in him to a son.

Though Dan, like Rosalie, was an only child, others had claimed his father's spiritual paternity and earthly attention. He'd never felt it, but he recognized his father in himself now, increasingly, in his preoccupation with life's evanescence. Not time—time was lost as well in the unknowable—but the spark that was known as Dan, the spark that danced near the spark that was Rosalie. If they had this less-than-a-moment's sentience, how much less lonely to share it? He had nothing like his father's brilliance to attract her. What did he have? He saw his apartment through her eyes, oppressive in its bleakness, as though whoever lived there was moving out, no object related to any other in meaningful proportion or color or orientation, leaving uneasy space where nothing could happen.

Rosalie lifted Nobu off her lap. The cat sharpened his claws on the bed's bare mattress. Later, Dan wondered why he'd let Rosalie go, or if he'd had a choice. She rose with a younger woman's ease, reclaimed her coat, and while Dan's lips were forming an invitation to dinner somewhere, anywhere, silenced him with a kiss so fleeting it might as well not have happened.

Chapter Eighteen

Hot Water

Juniper tautened her stomach muscles, conscious of Mikhail watching her step into the hot tub on his deck high over the river. The steaming water and the volcanic rocky soil and cliffs reminded her she had wanted to go to Iceland, but then she didn't, because everyone was going there, and the remote Iceland she wanted to see would have her camping with vagabonding backpackers. This was nicer. Besides, she felt too old for that now. She'd breathed Iceland's pure air once, in the 70s, when her student charter flight to London stopped in some sub-arctic airfield to refuel. The Iceland she craved was an Aurora Borealis in her soul. What she was finding with Mikhail was its antithesis, the dark sides of their souls entwined. She hadn't asked him yet about the mangled car at the end of his driveway. She doubted that was a story she wanted to hear, but if he didn't want to tell it, why had he invited her home and let her see the car's carcass accordioned against the tree trunk, like a perverse garden ornament?

Mikhail got into the hot tub behind her, pulled her onto his lap. Her breasts bobbed in the water. He feared it might be a failing in him, rooted in his family's Russian Old Believer ways, that he found such comfort in her abundance. He'd recreated himself, disavowing the icons and rituals, the anachronistic headscarves and beards. Sometimes he missed the way someone would always be singing, and the impulse to poetry survived in him. He'd intended to build a sauna like the ones he grew up with, too, but the hot tub beneath the stars was a good substitute.

Mikhail lived as close to the mountains as a person could, on the town's farthest fringes, his driveway the last before the National Forest began. It had seemed idyllic when he and Moira decided to build there, a summer decision made in happier times, severely strained by long winters and seldom-plowed roads complicating their commutes. They'd made concessions to financial and functional realities, the fireplace giving way to a wood-burning stove, one bedroom for the girls instead of two. Much that he'd intended to build remained unfinished. The house had worked well enough, though Moira never ceased complaining.

Juniper didn't seem the type to complain the way his wife had. Their bodies did most of the talking for them in their own language, an impetuous dialect. When he tried to translate it into words it made him nervous. Juniper didn't fit his template; the modern man he'd set out to become required blond perfection like Rosalie's. Here, tonight, without a witness, he could be whoever he wanted to be, and he wanted Juniper more than anything. She rolled on him beneath the water and he dove into her embrace.

CLIMBING OUT WET FELT TO JUNIPER LIKE BEING born again. Maybe this time she could avoid catastrophes. Some people seemed to take in immunity to catastrophe with their mother's milk. She'd thought she was one of them until she met Dakota. On the deck, Mikhail gave her a blanket and took one for himself. They sat in Adirondack chairs listening to the river. Mikhail could have no idea what resonance it had for her, soundtrack to the adventure movie her life had been for a decade. Mikhail was more like a cave than a river, hazardous and profound. The stars flew, startling above the pines.

AS MIKHAIL'S BODY COOLED, HIS MISGIVINGS kicked in. This was their third time together alone, and threes were numbers requiring caution. Three wishes, three wise men, too many for coincidence, too few for routine, the beginning of a pattern, or the end of a song. What did Juniper infer was going on between them? The debacle Mikhail had experienced taught him to pay attention to other people's judgment of his motives. He hummed a melody that had never made the pop charts. His own voice soothed him. As a child he'd sung in the children's choir, voices so soaring and pure his eyes teared, the closest he'd come to understanding what the elders meant he should call *God*.

Juniper admired Mikhail's voice, but she could feel him withdrawing from her.

"What's that you're singing?"

"Nothing."

Juniper was getting cold. She clutched the blanket around her shoulders and went inside to find her clothes. Mikhail's complacent old dog Boris was napping on her sweater. He rolled over in his sleep when she pulled it out from under him. Something had soured between her and Mikhail with nothing said. She'd seen no sign of post-coital melancholy in him before.

He followed her into the house and put on his jeans. He poured himself a drink and pointed the open bottle in her direction. "Vodka?"

"I've got to go. We're catering a funeral brunch tomorrow." Mikhail didn't try to stop her leaving. She tasted the vodka on his lips.

Chapter Nineteen

Blood Tells

Juniper was a good citizen—she let her smartphone go to voicemail rather than answer it as she drove. She went into the house and turned up the heat before she checked who'd called. She smiled to see it was River. He didn't call often. If he'd been grabbing a break between sets, she'd probably miss him when she called back, but no.

"Hey, Mom."

"Hey love, what's up?" She waited while he did whatever he needed to do with whatever he was watching on his laptop. She could always tell when someone's attention was divided on the phone.

"Okay, I was researching some music on YouTube." Long pause. Juniper shivered and pulled her coat closer around her neck, that feeling they called *someone walking over your grave*, but how could that be if you weren't dead? "You there, Mom?"

"I'm here."

"So, then I see *myself*, me as an old guy, in a wheelchair, with all these tattoos, but my face, my body, playing guitar the way I dream I could—some motivational crap video from Anchorage, but the music! I'll send you the link. Okay, call me crazy. It's a long shot here, but I'm wondering if there's something you need to tell me."

"Like what, for instance?" Juniper was shaking. This *was* crazy, impossible. The person she'd been a quarter-century ago was a stranger to her. Her summer impetuosity had been outside time. That was its beauty, its escape from loneliness, escape from the nagging weight of adult responsibility. With no future to it no one could be hurt, except that nature knows no time-out. Dakota had disappeared, comatose, into the aid car. When construction on the house next door recommenced, there was an entirely new crew. By the time she knew she was pregnant the builders were gone, the house was sold, and the new owners knew nothing. Greg was back soon enough to make her pregnancy plausible. *Just*. River couldn't mean what she thought he meant. She shouldn't catastrophize. *Breathe*. She'd make him spell it out. "What are you asking?"

"I don't look anything like you or Dad. Dad can't carry a tune; he's got no sense of rhythm. I hate camping—the only running water I like is a hot shower."

"You're not the first kid to be different from his father. You're not adopted."

"Mom, it's not just that I look like this guy, it's like I *know* him. I move like him, I sound like him.

And I'm not a kid at all anymore. I'm old enough to know where I came from."

"Bizarre coincidence. The birds and the bees, sweetheart." Juniper's heart hammered. She hoped he would hang up on her, but no. "You sound thirteen, fantasizing the hospital switched you at birth, so you don't have to be part of your geeky family."

"I won't tell Dad, I promise, even if he knows."

"Of course he doesn't know! I mean…"

"No do-overs, Mom. Truth time, now."

She knew he'd be relentless, no matter how she fought, and what was the point? He'd win in the end. It was easier than she'd expected to tell him her story, *his* story, in general terms. He listened without comment. Daily witness to excess and bad behavior in the casinos, River was hard to shock. Information is power and once he owned it, the question was, what would he do with it?

"I'm going to Alaska."

"What? No way!"

"Like a private investigator. Dad'll like that I want to go somewhere rugged."

"He'll want to go, too."

"I'll tell him I want my own adventure. He'll be proud of me for a change."

"And once you're there?"

"I'll find the man. I might hate him. I won't introduce myself until I know."

"You won't have to. He'll recognize you like looking in a mirror, maybe remember who your mother is if you give him some clues."

Juniper felt excitement fizzing off River through the phone when he said goodbye. Did she have anything to lose? Would it be so bad for Greg to feel pain? She hadn't known herself as vengeful until now. Releasing her secret was like taking off blinders, seeing the whole panorama, the scary edges she'd hidden from herself. The most important thing had been that River had a father, the next most important, that Greg had a son. She'd given them both what they needed to be happy, but that hadn't stopped Greg from running off with Glory. Afraid he would run off with River, too, she'd buried her hurt and made nice, as though Greg's deception and abandonment were forgivable. All along, she'd been the best mother she knew how to be.

Her own mother had done the best she could for Juniper, too, and it hadn't been very good. Juniper had determined to do better, and she had; her mother set a low bar. Juniper conjured a tall white house in a meadow, flowers all around, a man with flowing golden hair who tossed her in the air and kissed her, who may have been her father. Everyone in that house had long hair. When she tried to sort his features from the others in her memory they were lost in sunshine and sweet breezes that whirled their hair across their faces and made halos of it around their heads—a household of angels.

She hadn't known for a long time that she was supposed to have one mother and one father. She sorted out the mother part because while all the grownups came and went, she was the person who was there most. Sometimes they all sat down to picnics on the grass, with other children to play with, or feasts at long tables, where Juniper was passed from one lap to the next and fed bites of sautéed forest mushrooms or homemade ice cream. Sometimes everyone was drowsy and distracted, and she ate whatever she found in the cupboards she could reach.

She'd been four when she and her mother moved on and Daddy came into her life, a rodeo bull rider with a cowboy hat and a fancy silver belt buckle the size of a saucer. She learned to love him with all her heart. The thing he cared for more than her and her mother was riding bulls, and the money he won for them doing it. There was no big white house, no house at all. They lived on the road, first in a battered camper, then in an RV that felt like a palace in comparison. Juniper grew robust on rodeo fry bread and tacos and hot dogs on a stick. She was six when Daddy rode his last bull, out of the chute at the top of his game, then his hat blowing across the arena while she cheered from the bleachers for him to get up. Mama was willowy and vague in mourning, and her sad, dark beauty soon attracted Lloyd, who didn't mind she was a poor cook and housekeeper. He liked that she was sympathetic and undemanding.

They settled into Lloyd's rambler in Tacoma. Juniper accepted Lloyd's last name but spurned his overtures at fatherhood. Mama soon produced a brother for her, a child better suited to suburban life than she was, and the happy family was complete. Juniper's brother bored her from infancy. They were neither close nor unkind to each other. These were the days before cell phones and email; when Juniper left home, they kept in haphazard touch with postcards and holiday greetings. Her brother became a special ed teacher, married, had two children, and took early retirement, all within shouting distance of their childhood home. His idea of adventure was the annual family trip to Hawaii, which Juniper and Greg had endured one year for River's sake, then scrupulously avoided right up through their divorce. Mama's dementia went unnoticed, similar as it was to her normal interaction with the world, until she forgot her husband's name. One day her heart forgot to beat. Lloyd moved in with their son, the good child. No one expected anything of Juniper.

What was she supposed to do with this wretched freedom now, not even her secret to protect anymore?

The cat door flapped. Super Cat stomped in,

yowling for his dinner. At least her cats needed her. Juniper believed in indoor cats, but Super Cat disagreed in the extreme and was impossible to deny on either side of a door. She'd been fortunate to find a landlord with a mouse problem. When Butterball came along, with one cat constructively in residence, the precedent was set. Butterball was useless as a mouser. She'd arrived with a live-in human male, and stayed when her person moved on, much easier to live with than he'd been. Juniper fed the cats, then lay on the yellow loveseat with them, looking through tears at all the things she should clean and put in order. Her life for one.

Chapter Twenty

Left Early...

Dan touched his lips, reliving Rosalie's brisk good-bye kiss. She moved fast—her words, her body were quicksilver compared to his concrete. He had to be prepared next time. Newly trusting Nobu kneaded the futon while Dan laid his plans. Dan drowsed at two in the morning, then woke again at four and gave up on sleep. Rosalie had invited herself to his place for his cat's sake—he would appear at her door for the ostensible benefit of Roger the Dog. The creature had sabotaged their first tête-à-tête, now he'd be conscripted as ally in Dan's campaign for Rosalie. Dan tried slow breathing into his belly as he waited for sunrise, but that made the dark more viscous. He got up and brewed a pot of Lapsang. By the last smoky sip he was jiggling one leg over his knee. He took a longer shower than his frugality condoned. As he buttoned a clean shirt, the sky to the east announced the new day in an orange blast before spreading blue and clear, exactly what his plans required.

Dan's breakfast at the bakery up the street was

tasteless and dry in his mouth. Esteban didn't use last names in class, tango's physical intimacy protected by anonymity like AA's, *Hi, Rosalie! Hi, Dan!* Why hadn't he asked when he told her his, so he could at least search for her phone number? How do you do that nowadays? It was different when we still had landlines and directories. No, it would be too easy for her to refuse on the phone. Timing was critical to success—too early and Rosalie might be asleep, too late she'd be out.

He rang her doorbell at 9:03. Roger the Dog's lugubrious bark warned him off. How could Dan be nervous, he who'd approached uncounted dicey doors in his career? There'd been a logic to those approaches, though, an assigned job to be done. He'd followed his heart here to Rosalie's door, but he wasn't convinced his heart was a reliable or appropriate guide. The door opened.

"Dan?" Rosalie squinted at him through her uncombed hair, pulled it back with one hand, rubbed her eyes with the other. She stepped back as he stepped forward, the way they did in tango class. Dan amazed himself with his audacity. Rosalie hugged her robe around her and shushed the dog. "I'm not a morning person. I was just making coffee."

Dan saw he had the advantage. The morning light was harsh on Rosalie's bare face, lines around her mouth, a droop to her eyelids he'd overlooked before, her hands and arms coarsened by immoderate sun. Seeing her now, he admired the artfulness she employed to transform her public self. That she showed herself to him this way, undefended, pierced his heart. Though he was jangling from Lapsang, he left his shoes in the entry and followed her to the kitchen. While she performed the ritual dictated by her sophisticated espresso machine, Dan assessed the copper pans hanging from the overhead rack. Someday he would cook lavish breakfasts for Rosalie. He would stock the refrigerator to bursting with gourmet ingredients and grow herbs in pots on the windowsills.

THE ESPRESSO WAS RICH AND AROMATIC. As always for Rosalie, it put the day in focus, and what a strange beginning to it this was, with Dan at her kitchen counter as though he lived here. She was thankful it wasn't Mikhail who'd barged in and caught her in deshabille. She never went out without makeup—the habit of a lifetime, encouraged, if not actually demanded, by Howard. She hadn't showered yet, so she kept her distance from Dan. If she'd been more awake, she would have made some excuse to send him away.

DAN KNOCKED BACK THE ACID DRINK AND CLEARED his throat. Right on cue, Roger was sniffing his cuffs. "I was thinking Roger might like a hike this morning. There's a nice stretch of trail between

Penstemon and Wilder Falls."

"What a splendid offer!"

"Really?" Dan hadn't imagined it would be so easy, or feel so wonderful, to stir Rosalie's enthusiasm.

"Yes, he'd love it! I was feeling guilty he'd be alone all morning while I was out. Leave me your number to call when I get home. I'll give you lunch."

Dan tamed his grimace into a smile. Rosalie gave him the dog's leash and an ominous pocketful of plastic bags, and saw them off. Roger looked back startled when the door shut behind them, then gave the dog equivalent of a shrug and followed Dan to his car. The good side to this travesty was earning Rosalie's gratitude; the dismal side was everything else. She'd taken his words as spoken, too guileless to wonder what he meant. It was his own fault she'd misinterpreted his invitation. Not that Roger would ever tell if they didn't, but they might as well take that hike between the falls to work off Dan's caffeine palpitations.

Half a dozen cars shared the parking area at the lower falls trailhead. The hike upriver was Dan's initiation into apparent dog ownership. Roger's heavy jowls and broad torso implied an aggressive personality that couldn't have been further from the truth. They met as many dogs as people on the trail, and at each canine encounter Roger cowered rather endearingly behind Dan's legs. The human response was sympathy or condescension, which Dan found irritating. Roger's snuffling was irritating, too. Dan worried that the dog might drop dead on the trail from exertion. Then what would he tell Rosalie?

A mile on, the day's beneficence penetrated his sulk. Pungent sun-warmed cottonwood and willow buds dared to unfurl early and birds chorused, as confused by climate change's mixed signals as the humans were. It would have been immeasurably better shared with Rosalie. He might have taken her hand as they hiked. He'd tell her about it when he returned Roger. Dan's attitude improved, seeing the dog as his hostage to be exchanged later for Rosalie's attention and regard. Everything here was moving toward *life*, the birds hysterical with the will to propagate, young cattail reeds poking through marshland. Dan's feet felt lighter.

They evaded a mountain biker taking the descent from the second falls at full speed. Roger the Dog made the final uphill trudge grudgingly. At the fenced overlook shaded by tall pines Dan leaned on a log railing rubbed smooth by others' elbows. The churning water plunged over the volcanic cliffs as though it had volition of its own.

A man with a little boy joined them. "Awesome view, isn't it?"

Dan was torn between courtesy and alarm for the free-run boy who could easily slip through the railing or, alternatively, antagonize the dog by some silly gesture. He tried to keep an eye on both as he answered. "Hypnotic, hard to look away from all that energy."

The man grabbed the boy by the tail of his tee shirt. "You got to wonder how that guy who jumped off found the nerve to do it. I think maybe it wasn't from right here, though, probably over there where there's no rail. Clinically depressed and bankrupt, with the Great Recession and all. Crazy things happened then, but you got to admit it's a prime place for suicide."

Dan turned, nauseous at the thought, and nearly fell over Roger squatting behind him. Without witnesses he would have fled, but the little boy was watching. Dan wrapped a plastic bag over his hand and picked up the dog's stinking turd, trying not to breathe. Holding his breath added to his panic. He was seeing the distraught suicide leaping from the cliff, the few seconds in free-fall before gravity destroyed his illusions: he could never be free, merely dead. Dan's phone rang and went to voicemail while he tried to reach it with one hand and close the plastic bag with the other.

Dan and Roger backtracked into the sun. Once they'd gone far enough that he couldn't hear the waterfall, Dan sank onto a dry grass hummock and lowered his head between his knees. Slowly the sepia death-murk lifted, sounds and colors returned. He raised his head. Everything was there, tarnished but alive. Rosalie's voicemail said she was back—he could bring Roger home.

Rosalie looked both more, and less, like herself, dressed for the day. Now that Dan had seen the face beneath the face she showed the world, he couldn't un-see it. She seemed more real to him, not so much beyond his reach, yet his reach wasn't so long. Roger trundled past her into the house without fuss. Dan risked taking Rosalie's lunch invitation for granted and followed him.

In a media alcove off the entry, sirens blared from a TV. Rosalie muted it. "It was Paris this time. Paris again!" Colored lights flashed in surreal silence from police vans and ambulances; people ran, stumbling over bulky objects. "We're habituated. It's like during the Vietnam War when we watched people napalmed while our mothers gave us dinner. The reporters seem too sad to talk about what's happened, wherever they are, but they have to."

Dan turned away from a reporter interviewing a young, blood-spattered survivor, the hideous unthinkable become commonplace. "Our generation thought we'd change everything for the better."

Rosalie clicked off the picture. "Does anyone believe that now? Aren't we all shouting against the wind?"

Rosalie's home suggested serenity and balance were possible within its walls. Dan thought serenity would be a good beginning—affection, whatever happiness he retained capacity to feel. He had scant comfort to proffer on the subject of human nature. "Have you tried turning off the news?"

"Too much bleak curiosity. I read apocalyptic novels, too. Gruesome things. We need extreme atrocities in fiction so we can tell ourselves things aren't that bad, not yet. Do we hate ourselves? Are we all about our own destruction in the end? Is that what we are as a species?" Roger had been listening beside Dan, fidgeting with equally growing discomfort. He whined. Rosalie caressed his ears. "Sorry, sorry to go off. You two must be hungry. I'll fix our lunch."

The darkness Dan had been fighting since his conversation at the waterfall made eating a questionable prospect, but Rosalie's idea of "fixing" was about as nominal as her idea of "lunch." The kale chips with hummus congealed in his stomach. The New Zealand sauvignon blanc she poured was more welcome.

Rosalie toasted him in ironic celebration. "Another day in paradise. I feel like I'm cheating. We're so spoiled, untested." Dan didn't feel untested, but he didn't contradict her. She didn't pause to let him. "I try to imagine living through a disaster, feeling terror like that."

"Not so different, a matter of degree. Why would you want to know?"

"To feel alive! Could I bear it? Fighting to survive, not a placeholder for something more authentic."

"Suffering is more authentic?"

"Think of mothers and children in war zones, how strong they have to be."

"Men and boys, too."

"It's what males do anyway. If they weren't ducking bombs and shooting each other they'd be fighting over football or women."

"You have a low opinion of men."

"Present company excluded."

"Really?"

Rosalie laughed and tapped Dan's arm. "No, what makes you any different?"

"I don't fight with other men, only with myself."

"Do you win?"

Everything in Dan was straining toward Rosalie, to hold her, to show her this was as real as life needed to be, but he could be forbearing, respectful, try to win her heart and mind before her body. "Sometimes. If the worst that can happen has, it makes it easier not to be afraid. Or that's what I used to think." He hadn't intended saying it aloud, or maybe he had, to draw her to him out of sympathy for his own unimaginable tragedy, to play on her guilt feelings if she refused him.

Rosalie paused with a kale chip halfway to her mouth. "But you don't think so now."

"I'm always afraid there'll be a new worst, not just for me specifically, for other people, the whole world."

"That's grim thinking, too."

"A lot of that going around."

Their conversation drifted into nullity. Dan guessed she found him self-dramatizing. He kept his report on his hike with Roger prosaic. It was a bad day to be alone; he lingered longer than he might have otherwise. In the moment after Rosalie put their plates in the dishwasher, rinsed her hands, and turned to him, the hair rose on Dan's arms. She might be silently consenting to his unspoken desire. Or she might not be. He did nothing.

Rosalie sighed. "I have work to do, Dan. I'd better get to it. I'll see you at the milonga. And let me know when you want to borrow Roger again."

Chapter Twenty-One

Girl Talk

Tourists flocked like starlings to the cafés in the old downtown's few square blocks, outdoor tables warmed in the morning sun. Juniper was sure she made a dull target for local fauna observers on her way to work. She was surprised to see Rosalie outside her favorite coffee house, the pretentious one where baristas spooned the ground beans onto an electronic scale, adding a little or brushing a bit off to meet their epicurean standards. Juniper wondered if it made a difference, but they gave a good show and strong mocha. She'd never seen Rosalie there before. Neither was dressed the way they normally knew each other—Rosalie in sunglasses, fleece, and lycra, with a bored bulldog at her feet, Juniper in black shirt and pants with chunky black shoes. Rosalie did a double take, seeing her. Juniper knew the outfit made her look overstuffed and masculine. "My catering uniform. Attractive, huh?"

"It's nice on you."

Juniper recognized Rosalie's lie as a friendly gesture. She took the other chair at her table. "Adorable dog." That was a lie, too. The dog was drooling on the paving bricks, too lazy to lift its head.

Rosalie gave him a nudge with her trainer toe. He grunted without opening his eyes. "Roger's a bit sleepy. Dan took him on a hike yesterday and I'm afraid he expected more stamina from him."

"Dan from the dog, or the dog from Dan?"

Rosalie laughed. A man at the next table ogled her until he probably realized she was his mother's age. "Oh, I think Dan has plenty of stamina."

Did she mean what Juniper thought she meant? "You and Dan are *friends* now?"

"Like, you know, tango friends. He's taken a shine to Roger the Dog."

"Funny, I thought Dan was a cat person."

"You've met his cat?"

Did Rosalie think she had a thing going with Dan? Did she care? "We were both brushing cat hair off our clothes at class." This conversation involved more meaningless lies and evasions than Juniper typically told in a week. She turned her face toward the sun, sipped her mocha and changed the subject. "Ah, my drug of choice."

"Mine, too, one of them at least. I couldn't get through my days without it."

"You don't look like your days would be hard to get through." Juniper didn't mean to sound envious.

"They are, though. This is a new life for me. I'm trying to make sense of it. I don't sleep well, do you?"

Juniper hadn't last night. One confidence deserved another, but she couldn't tell Rosalie about River and Dakota. "Better than I used to. I used to worry about living alone, about bad guys waiting in the alley ready to crawl through my windows and steal all my stuff and murder me. Then it sunk in that big money interests were feeding my fear so I'd buy stuff to feel better. I think of myself as *someone*, but to them we're cattle."

Rosalie looked bemused, or maybe amused at her rant. "Cattle, really?"

"It's blatant—look at the media. I'm not some paranoid conspiracy nutcase."

"You don't strike me as a nutcase."

"How do I strike you?"

"Different, unusual."

"I can't help that. I've never known the rules, always making it up as I go along, wondering how regular people live their lives. Everybody who was supposed to teach me those things disappeared or lost their minds or died."

Juniper broke off. Their conversation was evolving into the reckless intimacy of women on a plane, or a bus, or in a hospital waiting room. Rosalie had started telling a story while Juniper's attention stayed mired in her own. Against her better judgment, Juniper tuned back in.

"… I'm not sure I'm sorry I wasn't with him in the end. Like I said, I try to make sense of it, and maybe there's no sense to be made. Was it up to me to see him out? He set up his own life, his choices weren't my responsibility. I'm rambling; I don't mean to sound cold."

Whatever Rosalie had been talking about, Juniper agreed with her on principle. "We're all responsible for our own, aren't we? Choices, I mean. Unless everything that happens is predestined, *meant to be*."

Rosalie groaned at the cliché. Not a high note to end on, but Juniper checked the time. "Oops, gotta run! See you at the milonga, for sure."

Rosalie lingered over her empty cup, wondering why she'd improvised that lie about Howard's dying in a mountain crevasse. What if the others compared notes? But why pollute this sun-filled morning with the stench of Howard's sick room? She worried about her recurrent urge to confess. She didn't deserve the relief of confession. Penance, atonement, was what she owed. What would that look like? Rosalie didn't feel better for the conversation. She hadn't been her best self. She smiled at the man at the next table. He made a show of consulting his phone.

Chapter Twenty-Two

Easy Come...

Esteban's standard of living—he couldn't call it a lifestyle, given it had no style at all—rose with the Argentina trip deposit from the white-haired couple. He still slept in his car, but thanks to them, he was eating better. He stuck to takeout to cut the tip expense. He bought himself new underwear. He'd been going without for economy's sake, not transgressive thrill. He bought a new shirt at the outlet mall and saved it for next week's milonga.

Friday morning, the steam over the indoor city pool melted the chill from his bones. He pretended he was in the Caribbean again, except that the air smelled of chlorine rather than jasmine bloom, and the skin his skimpy Speedos exposed had long faded from tanned to pallid. A woman, more a girl, in a green one-piece was watching him flex his shoulders, no doubt expecting him to slice a smooth dive into the deep end. He hated to do it, but he eased into the water feet first, holding onto the edge. One of the few ways he disappointed women—he liked to think the only way, though his numerous ex-lovers might argue the point—was that he couldn't dive, could barely swim a pool's length. He subtly exhibited other assets poolside. They called men's swimming briefs "budgie smugglers" in Australian slang. With Aussie women he'd always gotten a laugh, and often more, when he guaranteed he wasn't smuggling budgies. American women missed the point entirely; he had to fall back on the old not-a-banana Mae West reference.

The girl in the green swimsuit tempted him. Naturally he'd be faithful to Aurelia, but they hadn't met yet, had they? When they did, he would give up one-night stands, one-week ones, too, but for now he had no confidante, no playmate, and frankly he craved a night in a warm bed. He rested a moment, floating on his back. The girl tied a towel around her hips. He might not look impressive in the water, but his muscular arms and abs showed to advantage as he hoisted himself out to stand dripping near her.

Esteban doubted the girl had seen the twenty-one years she claimed, but she said she didn't live with her parents, and had a car of her own. He was positive she wasn't underage. She picked him up that evening at the town's best mountain-view hotel. He didn't have to lie to her, she took care of that in her personal reality script. She wasn't experienced enough with the traveling world to wonder why he'd swim at the city pool when his hotel had its own. Her unworldliness, however, didn't extend to her expectations of how a man should treat her. She knew her way around well enough to land them in a cacophonous modernist restaurant with entree prices that could have fed him for a week—more with appetizers and wine. At least he got off with the cheapest vintage. Either she didn't mind, didn't know the difference, or didn't want to push her luck with his generosity before dessert. She also didn't know how little he left for a tip, sure he'd never be back to face the server's disdain.

For the meal's price he could have gotten a warm room in a tolerable motel with clean sheets. The girl's hair conditioner and perfume made a poisonous duo that failed to mask the fact she wasn't into doing laundry, something he couldn't have known at the pool, where everyone smelled the same. In her bedroom she lit a scented candle that added to the fug. Esteban knew himself as a man, men as weak creatures, vulnerable to visual stimuli, and as he'd guessed, what the girl's modest swimsuit had hidden was visually stimulating indeed. For fifteen minutes he indulged his other senses, putting smell on hold. In the spirit of fair trade he made sure she got what she'd bargained for. Afterwards he moaned in ecstasy at stretching full-length for a long sleep. He woke alone to angry female voices. The girl returned to hustle him into his clothes and out through a mercilessly bright living room, where her roommate scowled like an avenging deity. The girl dropped him at the hotel without apology before midnight. He'd told her he was from Rio, passing through on business, the story a careless, shortsighted means to his ends. The next weeks at the pool could be awkward.

Chapter Twenty-Three

The Other Side of the Glass

Mikhail traced Juniper's passage through her cottage by lights going on from room to room. Her gray cat froze with one paw raised, seeing him in the moonless garden, then crept away. The cat would tell no tales. Mikhail made a knight's move for a better view through the bedroom window. This wasn't the first time he'd watched her. If he paused to think about it, he felt ashamed; he wasn't that class of man, not a peeping Tom type at all. That was a perversion, so he didn't think about it. Juniper was to blame for not lowering her blinds. They hadn't spoken in the forty-eight hours since their evening in his hot tub, and Mikhail had meant to leave it that way. He'd stopped himself from knocking on her door the night before, but he'd—utterly by fluke—seen her inside, dancing, and become an invisible audience to her solo performance. She'd drawn him here again tonight and he'd come softly, so she wouldn't see him, so he could turn around halfway down her walk and leave, as his better judgment told him to do. But he didn't.

Juniper found solace playing with her clothes, composing her closet by colors like a painting, weeding the outworn to clear her mind, trying new ensembles to dream. Also to mourn. She stripped off the caterer's uniform and the mannishness it imposed, revealing the entertaining underwear she wore as her private rebellion, freed her braid, and bent over, brushing her hair until it unfurled, electric as a thundercloud. She draped herself in a scarlet kimono, silk against skin, struck a pose in her full-length mirror. She was too hungry. She went to find carnal comfort in the kitchen, gleanings from the evening's reception where "heavy *hors d'oeuvres*" had proven less popular than the alcohol on offer. Salmon and goat cheese baked *en croute*, asparagus spears in bacon, herbed game hen legs, radishes and baby carrots no one ever ate, lemon bars for dessert—all finger food. She wouldn't have to wash a dish. Super Cat slunk in through the cat flap and nipped her ankles. She dropped him some bacon and wiped her fingers to answer her phone. She recognized the breathing. Her stomach knotted. "Mikhail, where are you?"

"Where do you think?"

Juniper opened her door. "Why don't you knock like a normal person?"

"I like to be invited in."

"Come in, then, you're in time to eat."

Super Cat growled and left a greasy trail, dragging his bacon under the table. Mikhail spread his arms wide; Juniper dodged his embrace. He shrugged and produced his vodka flask. She wouldn't give him the satisfaction of knowing about the new bottle in her freezer. She'd bought it on impulse, conjuring a future through the rising haze of sexual intoxication, but she knew he was treacherous precisely *because* they were soul mates. She could trust him no more than she could trust herself.

Her daydreams had veered north when she followed River's link to Dakota's music, telling herself it couldn't be, but it *was*, him, hair standup red as she remembered it, face as grooved as the dissipated rock star he'd never become, those tattoos crawling up his creased neck. Hunched in his wheelchair, Dakota channeled a vast arctic loneliness, compressed it into notes and chords, and tore them from his guitar strings. Now River would be there, too, her boy, far from his interfering stepmother and Greg.

Mikhail seemed suburban against that drama, and if her attitude could change so precipitously, his could, too. She'd be a fool to expect anything enduring with him—if she even wanted it. That she'd had the misfortune to be in love with her husband, yet faithless, had skewed every relationship since, but some mistakes were not irreparable. Juniper laid out the leftovers on the coffee table. She ate appreciatively, taking big bites as she always did, but the food brought no comfort, nor did Mikhail beside her, her thigh pressing his because the loveseat was narrow. She wouldn't admit her desire to be close to him.

MIKHAIL SMELLED GARLIC IN JUNIPER'S HAIR AND on her skin, sour saltiness from inside her kimono, where she'd yet to wash off the day's anxiety. He watched her sidelong through the lens of not-so-bygone desires. She was missing only an apron to play to his youthful fantasies, when he'd dreamed of the Old Believer girls' long dresses loosed, primly braided hair undone, coming to him like this with food and barely veiled nakedness. And the One he'd fallen in love with, a second cousin from their sect's tiny inbred community—eighteenth-century Russia in 1970s Oregon. He'd loved in her the purity he'd imagined despoiling, but he'd been judged too much *estranged*, with too much secular education, too little devotion to their religion's rituals and rules, eating from anyone's dishes, no longer "in union." He was scarcely sanctioned to pray in their onion-domed church, and certainly not to marry in it. He'd been raised with his nose pressed against the glass between himself and the world he'd been told was a hostile place, yet his own community had betrayed him.

His marriage to Moira had been vengeance on his people who'd written him off, and it had been a fiasco. He'd foresworn any subsequent attachment that would bind him, but nights alone had grown intolerable. His heart hurt, and now his vodka flask was empty. He ached to anchor himself in Juniper. They fit together. He could stop struggling—through her he would understand his place in the world. She was as impatient as he was with ordinary propriety. No matter how she tried to hide herself behind chaos and clutter, disguise herself in gaudy costume, he would excavate her secrets, make them—and her—his, and give himself to her, wholly. He pushed aside Juniper's eating hand, buried his head in her lap, and sobbed like a child.

Juniper wasn't accustomed to emotional outbursts by men. Anger or desire's urgency, laughter or frustration, sure, but men she'd known didn't cry. She held a lemon bar aside with one hand and petted Mikhail's hair with the other, finger-combing it over the thin spot, usually invisible due to his height, until his sobs stopped. Without raising his head he nuzzled the opening in her kimono and licked his tears' salt from her thighs. There, more evidence they were fatally two of a kind. She elbowed him away. "Go home, Mikhail. You're drunk. I'm tired, I need to sleep."

"We can sleep."

"Alone. I need to sleep alone."

He stood swaying like a bewildered bull. Juniper stood with him. It would be effortless to comfort him with an honesty of the body that would be a dishonesty of the heart. She couldn't erase what she'd done before she met him by pretending it didn't matter. She had to live it out. Settling for anything less would be spiritual slumming. She had to believe she was better than that.

Mikhail gathered her to him, his arms around her tender. He whispered against her ear. "Next time, then."

"Uh-huh, next time."

Chapter Twenty-Four

Milonga

Esteban created magic for his Tuesday night milonga. Magic was what everybody wanted. Tango was no ordinary dance, and those who came seeking it sought more than recreation; whether they knew it or not, they yearned for enchantment. He began with folding chairs and card tables from the Norwegians' storeroom arranged around the hall's edges.

The shamrocks gone, he'd had to mine the Dollar Store for decoration. He'd humbled himself to go there before, for deodorant, batteries, necessities a person living in his car couldn't expect to be fussy about. Off the highway strip that looked unappealingly Anywhere, America, if not for the snow-covered volcanoes gleaming in the distance, the store was a paean to Chinese manufacture and the universal human taste for shiny things. Winter-themed doodads were marked down, but Esteban was sick of cold feet and long dark hours. His milonga would be all about spring—pastel paper tablecloths, matching napkins and cups, artificial daffodils in plastic vases, battery-powered candles that "burned" magenta and green and yellow, effervescent water bottled to look like Perrier, bags of cookies—a new hole sprung in his flimsy financial lifeboat.

By seven-thirty, lights dimmed and candles flickering beneath daffodil bouquets on each table, the hall looked, if not like a special place, like a place where something special could happen. Esteban muttered a prayer to the tango gods and started the music, a Juan d'Arienzo tango, cheerful and energizing—a piece you couldn't *not* dance to. Dan came first, right on schedule. The other five students dribbled in one by one. While they found seats and changed their shoes, a new couple arrived, then two more women and a man. Esteban could breathe again. He herded his six onto the dance floor. They didn't look too bad for beginners, and they circled decorously in the counter-clockwise line of dance, causing no problems for the new arrivals, who had clearly tangoed with one another before. Esteban exercised his cruise-ship diplomacy, inviting the extra woman to dance a tanda. She was young, tattooed, and her black pants hung precariously low on her slim hips. She had enough experience to appreciate his superb lead.

As host, he kept an eye on the door. In the first half hour the paid admissions covered his Dollar Store costs. He'd take a shot at recruiting to fill Aurelia's class from among the fresh blood. Two more young men arrived, exchanging high-fives and hugs with the woman with the low-slung pants while Esteban collected their money. His students appeared to be figuring things out for themselves; he'd taught them enough to do it.

Outside in his car, Mikhail had fortified himself with vodka. He'd promised himself he'd wait until after the milonga, his promise as worthless as he knew it would be. He was excited by the thought of dazzling the women with his masterful lead. Along with that came stage fright, ergo the vodka. He'd refilled his flask from the bottle under the seat and salvaged some inner dignity by saving the rest for later. Thrown for a moment by the dim lights and flickering candles inside the hall, he calmed seeing familiar faces—that white-haired couple, who were such a nation of two he'd never caught their separate names, and Dan changing into his smooth-soled shoes.

Seeing Juniper stirred an uncomfortable incomplete memory, or dream residue. He remembered hiding behind the shrubs watching her undress. And the cat. When was that? He'd gone in, he thought, and eaten something with Juniper, or had he? Hadn't he meant to avoid her? He was left with an unpleasant hollowed-out feeling without detail to explain it. Juniper wore a short pink dress and crystal earrings like chandeliers, her hair pinned up with bits falling in the front on each side—a down-market diva, transcending ordinary taste. Before Mikhail could greet her properly, Esteban propelled them onto the dance floor. Mikhail's life was baffling, distressing in many ways, but he felt indomitable in tango—he could forget all his torment and merge with this fabulous woman for the space of a song.

Juniper had considered skipping the milonga even as she was dressing for it. Though she hadn't bought the ticket yet, her life here, and Mikhail, seemed already past. Nostalgia was useless. Instead, she pictured herself repairing the damage she'd wrought in Dakota's life, and in River's. No, who was she kidding? If she were to "repair" anything it would be the course her own life had taken, into tedium broken by orgasm and wistful pretense at romance. She'd enticed Dakota with beer and sex for her own gratification. He might have toppled off the ladder anyway. She would never know. The choices she'd made in those few minutes weighed on her. She'd lacked the moral boldness to follow his ambulance.

She should have been with Dakota when he woke. She should have fronted up to Greg about Dakota, and to Dakota about their son. She could have weathered the consequences, no matter how things fell out. She'd chosen a life in service to her secret, finding her purpose and succor in the family that was Dakota's unwitting gift to her. She'd been a self-serving fantasist. Her secret gave her the excuse to be lackadaisical—to risk nothing means to lose nothing. If that meant she would *have* nothing either, wasn't that what she'd told herself she deserved?

Perhaps she was the last person Dakota wanted to see again. Perhaps she'd been erased from his memory, but she'd raised him a son she was belatedly willing to share. That had to buy her the right to make reparations, to say to him, face-to-face, *I'm sorry*, cleanse her soul and free herself for a future.

The new dress in her closet had persuaded her to come to the milonga. She couldn't foresee she'd have much occasion to wear a rose satin sheath in Alaska. She'd heard every city in the world had a tango community. That sounded like hyperbole, but she hoped for one in Anchorage. If her other emotions felt confused, she was clear about one new love—she'd fallen hard for tango.

With no time to warm up, she was graceless at first. Mikhail's hand on her back pressed her into closer connection, more to declare their bodies' intimacy than for the sake of the dance, she thought. She pulled away, not far enough to break the contact between follow and lead, but enough to assert her independence. No one else could see the struggle of wills going on in the millimeters between them.

Juniper dreaded Mikhail asking why she'd booted him out when he needed consolation. She didn't want a breakup scene, couldn't stomach seeing Mikhail cry again. She wasn't sure her explanation would hold up in so many words, or if they had anything to break up.

He was so handsome in his rumpled linen jacket, she wondered if she'd have the good sense, or the will, to refuse him again tonight. The fabric belonged to a warmer season, but they were creating an illusion of Buenos Aires here, weren't they? The dancing would soon make them all too warm, despite the chill that had returned to the mountains. She figured the jacket was rumpled because of Mikhail's careless housekeeping rather than any fashion-forward sense. Partly to head off his questions, partly for pure guilty pleasure, she yielded to his embrace. Several times Mikhail seemed about to speak when they moved apart between songs—his brows rose and he smiled, then let his smile fade, apparently having an internal conversation with himself, not sharing it with her.

The Broadway-themed *cortina* signaled the tanda's end. Time to change partners. Mikhail squeezed Juniper's hand, leaving her at her table. She squeezed back, *Later.* What harm could one more night do? She tried a *cabeceo* on Dan, who avoided her, maybe because she towered over him in her Argentine three-inch heels. Instead, he approached the white-haired woman, her husband having struck up a conversation with a newcomer. Mikhail led Rosalie onto the floor, and Juniper feared she'd be left a wallflower. Even more frightening, a stranger asked her to dance. It was fair to warn him. "I'm a beginner at this. I apologize in advance."

He smiled and lifted his left hand, palm up, in invitation to her right. "We're all beginners. Some of us have been beginners longer than others, that's all."

Juniper walked backwards easily in his close embrace, guided into steps she didn't know she knew. The man was plumpish, shorter, something oniony he'd had for dinner underlying his cologne, and he'd missed a spot near his ear when shaving. To Juniper in the dance he was none of that; they weren't two people, two genders even: they were only a good tanda's bliss.

DAN WAS INTRIGUED BY JUNIPER'S APPEARANCE. He wasn't one to go to extremes. This was a small event in a small town, where to him dressing up meant putting on freshly laundered khakis. He had to admit, Juniper's exuberance made him smile. He would dance with her, eventually. Rosalie had taken the opposite tack to Juniper. In simple black, she was her own adornment. Her hair curled soft and bright around her face, and her blue eyes glittered like jewelry. Dan found her restraint beguiling. He blessed Esteban's pairing him and Rosalie for the first tanda with no initiative on his part.

When the music began and he took her in his arms he was startled to find the black dress left Rosalie's back bare wherever he put his hand, skin on skin. He felt around, then affected not to notice. They circled the room with reasonable efficiency. Esteban had warned that talking was for the times *between* dances in the tanda, not for during them. At the first pause, Dan told Rosalie that Nobu was behaving like a normal cat ever since her visit. He liked talking with her about domestic things, but after the second song he knew he had to take the leap before someone else did. In the end it was easy. He asked if she might be interested in going for a drink after the milonga. She said that might be nice. The music started again, and for Dan the third dance was a triumphant lap in his personal Olympics. When they finished dancing, his hands smelled of her perfume.

Dan trusted his invitation to surround Rosalie like an invisible shield. According to milonga etiquette he had to release her to dance with others. He chose new partners at random, stuck to the several steps he'd practiced, squaring corners that were supposed to be round, looking at his feet, which Esteban had forbidden. Dan believed he could get better at this. He loved the warm embrace of tango, heart-to-heart, like the best parts of life.

His follows were tolerant. They may have heard the same wisdom Esteban quoted—the ungainly lead may eventually morph into someone you'd want to dance with, and leave you sitting if you've refused him in his inglorious past. Every woman Dan led helped him fill the wasteland before the last tanda that evening and whatever more the night held for him and Rosalie.

Rosalie wondered if Dan would make his move tonight at last, or had *that* been his move? His lukewarm approach rattled her self-assurance. Was he organizing an after-party, inviting all the women? Was he toying with her, or having second thoughts? Second thoughts sounded like Dan. Was he so fastidious that touching her bare back had put him off? Stepping onto the dance floor with her uncertain skills felt like being naked in public, but she'd looked good to herself in the mirrors at home, demure. She would have had to go over the top to compete with Juniper's getup, splashing out in questionable taste, a tango glamour parody. Juniper was a gender-bending, Wonder Woman type, impossible to get in definitive view. She changed with her costumes, different from other people who stayed who they appeared to be—out of step or a step ahead. This morphing quality was exasperating to Rosalie, who wanted always to be winning even a non-existent race. Bad enough being subsumed into Juniper's cartoonish world by association. How did you compete with a shape-shifter? Much better going for easy sophistication, never wrong in black, and more arresting for the contrast.

A new young couple arrived, she a 1940s film ingénue incarnate, he self-assured and noble of profile. They spun in the line of dance with unself-conscious dips and little kicks, embellishments Rosalie had seen in videos. Had she ever been so in love and lighthearted? She'd had her chance. Time was stealing the person she knew as herself, but she felt ageless in the tango, the center of her lead's attention, rapt in the music.

MIKHAIL ZIPPED QUICKLY WHEN DAN CAME INTO the restroom. Dan had diminished him from their first class. Mikhail was taller and better looking, younger, a better dancer by far, yet Dan had a solidity he envied. Not that there was much to him, but Dan seemed undeniably *himself*. Mikhail took his time washing his hands, and when Dan took his place at the sink, produced his flask and offered it.

DAN FELT GIDDY AS AN ADOLESCENT ANTICIPATing his first date. This furtive drinking in the toilets fit right in. He took a good-sized swig and returned it to Mikhail, who did the same, then handed it back without wiping the top. Dan wanted to tell

Mikhail he was going out with Rosalie, elated, not gloating, but the vodka drowned his words. They drank more, then Mikhail capped the flask, hid it in his jacket pocket, winked, and left without a word.

Words weren't coming easily to Mikhail this evening, no poetry tripping off his tongue. It didn't matter, *tango* was poetry. He scanned the room to find a partner. The girl with the sexy pants caught his eye; he liked her until he realized she reminded him of his daughters, and was about their age. That hurt. Of all his pain, losing his daughters' love was the worst. Moira knew it. It was her doing that they never called him, never picked up when he called their numbers, missing them, trying for a chance to make things right. How could he know what they needed from him if, on his few visits, they flanked their mother, the gorgon whose look could turn him to stone.

He would have danced with Juniper again if she hadn't been taken by another new lead. She was at least half a head taller than nearly all the men there, but he'd hardly seen her sitting. Surprisingly, Rosalie was, in a dim corner, alone. That wasn't right.

Dan bumped into Esteban, who was videoing the dancers with his phone. On the off chance the video was for Beatriz, or rather "Aurelia," Dan kept his face averted. He hadn't changed so much she wouldn't recognize him, even with glasses and without the trim beard he'd worn then. His vigilance was reflexive—what difference would it make now? He was no longer a presence in her world, and for all he could see she'd moved on, too. That said, some people's grudges knew no rational bounds, and Raoul and his thugs may not have found his retirement credible. Off in a corner, he saw Rosalie standing to dance with Mikhail again, twice this evening, though he wasn't exactly counting. Jealousy wasn't necessary; she'd be leaving with him, whether Mikhail knew it or not.

Esteban's video *was* for Aurelia. She didn't need to know which dancers were or weren't his students. It wasn't a lie to let someone make assumptions. The two young lovers doing *sacadas* and *voleos* and *ganchos* in the middle of the floor so as not to disrupt the line of dance might have been cast for the role. Mikhail and Rosalie made a handsome couple as long as he caught them when they weren't talking as they danced, and some of the visitors were good infill between the two extremes. He stopped shooting when Dan chugged into view leading the young woman with the tatts, doing a passable job, given his limited experience, but not something to brag about. Esteban had warned Dan against keeping his head down, but this was a milonga, a social dance, not a class or práctica, so he couldn't march out there and correct him. Esteban hummed along with the music, Donato's *Con Tus Besos,* With Your Kisses, in search of his next prospective tour member.

MIKHAIL HAD EXTRACTED ROSALIE FROM HER corner. "What are you doing sitting in the shadows? The most enticing woman in the room, alone?"

"Waiting for my prince, perchance."

"Your Highness, I believe they're playing our *vals.*"

Mikhail flouted the rule about not talking while they danced. "You were in my dream last night."

"Should I feel flattered?"

"I dreamed I was dancing with an iridescent bird." The poetry, sweet lies, returning. He'd been weak with Juniper, he'd do better with Rosalie.

ROSALIE CRINGED AT WHATEVER SHE'D DONE, OR had done to her, in Mikhail's dream, shaped to his desires, no doubt. The dreamed-of had no power, the dreamer no control, and thus was blameless. The indiscretion lay in revealing the dream's existence. But if, as she feared, she'd grown grotesque with age, what did she have to lose? Dan hadn't given her a glance since his comment about drinks. Rosalie and Mikhail had gotten off to an unpromising start, but his overt attraction to her tonight offered a way back to herself, or at least a way to hold her place—the Fred Astaire illusion, you and your partner alone and perfect in the universe. In the pause after the first song she shone her smile up at Mikhail; he reflected her allure back to her in his. By the second piece in the *vals* tanda more dancers had arrived, the floor was crowded, the circle moved slowly. As they reached the far end of the hall, Mikhail swept Rosalie in quick side steps around stacked chairs and an upright piano, out the rear exit to a patio waiting for summer. He led her in another turn, then leaned against an upended picnic table and drew her close.

"You know, a whole life can turn on a tanda."

Rosalie chuckled and nestled against his chest. "Dramatic, aren't you? It's freezing out here. I can see my breath."

"Try this."

Rosalie accepted Mikhail's small flat flask and tipped it up. "It's empty."

"I have more in my car."

"Are you suggesting we behave badly?"

"Very badly." Mikhail slid his hands beneath Rosalie's dress.

Rosalie slithered against Mikhail, teasing him like poking an animal with a stick, not caring that he might be dangerous. Mikhail fumbled with her dress, pulling it into order, breathing hard. "Come away with me."

"I have to get my coat."

"Meet me out front, I don't want to go back inside." Mikhail boosted himself over the low patio wall and disappeared around the building.

Rosalie sidled past the dancers in the *vals* tanda's last throes. She hastily snatched her things from the chair where she'd left them and stole off before the music stopped.

DAN GOT THE TANGO's *BUM-bum-BUM-bum* rhythm, but the three-quarter-time tango *vals* stymied him. The young woman unlucky enough to be his follow tolerated his efforts through all three songs. He would have given up, but he couldn't think how to do it without seeming rude, and evidently she couldn't either. He concentrated hard on his feet and thanked her with chagrin when they parted at the *cortina*. He was heading for Juniper's reassurance when he saw her accepting Esteban—luckily, since this turned out to be a fast-paced, confusingly named *milonga* tanda. Dan poured himself a paper cup of water and surveyed the dance floor, searching for Rosalie. He hoped she hadn't been watching his less-than-stellar *vals*.

He didn't see her anywhere, perhaps she was hidden by a lead. No, not on the dance floor. Her street shoes were tucked neatly paired beneath the chair where she'd left them when she changed into her stilettos, but her handbag was gone. She'd be in the ladies' then, maybe taking a break from other men's approaches. Dan chastised himself for not being more attentive. He would have to learn where the line lay for Rosalie between solicitous and overbearing. He needed a break himself; the room felt stifling. He couldn't account for the bad feeling invading him except that he was overheated from the dance. The night air in the parking lot, cold as a reprise of winter, revived him. Rosalie's car was there, parked near his among the other earliest arrivals'.

Panic nibbled at Esteban's composure. His edges were fraying. No one could tell by looking at him; he hadn't sweated through his shirt or gone white around the eyes. He'd been exultant at the turnout—so many candidates for his pitch about the trip to Argentina. He spread his charm lavishly, danced with the new women, and used the pauses in each tanda to cajole his follows with his Buenos Aires visions. Between tandas he regaled the men with tango adventures he made up on the spot, and lied about the extraordinary discount his colleague the tango *maestra* was offering for friendship's sake. He failed on every count, not least because many of the guests had been to Argentina, some for visits lasting months, and knew more about the Buenos Aires tango scene, and its prices, than he did. Others professed poverty, or family or work obligations, or were in town for a ski vacation then off to Switzerland, or they preferred the tango festivals in Portland, where the Argentinean teachers came to them. Esteban kept smiling but his face grew rigid with the effort as the evening went on. His fervor for Aurelia infected him like a tropical disease, a microbe inflaming his gut, eating him from the inside, she herself his only remedy. Touching her, being seen by her, was all he could think of now. Whatever happened afterward was up to the Fates.

It was plain to Juniper that Esteban's aplomb was pretense. His stressing out seemed strange when his evening was an obvious success, everyone else having a good time. She wanted to help him enjoy it a little. He complimented her on her progress, which was nice, except she could hear in his voice he wanted something from her. She'd discounted Rosalie's throwaway remark about his interest in her. She was too old and too large to be his type, though his type boundaries might flex with serious incentive. He was ridiculously good-looking—she felt his muscles in all the right places through his shirt when they danced—and he was the last thing she needed. He set her mind at ease on that count when he brought up the trip to Buenos Aires. She mentally edited his come-on: *a couple of spaces left* meant he needed more people to make it pay; *only the best dancers* meant he was asking everybody; *amazing discount price* meant he didn't know she couldn't possibly afford it, and his casual attitude showed he was at the end of his tether. Telling him she'd love to go bought her two more good *milonga* dances with him. It wasn't strictly a lie; she *would* love to go. He'd be happier for her saying so. That was a good thing, wasn't it?

Chapter Twenty-Five

Venus

Dan caught Juniper coming off her tanda with Esteban and led her into the next tango before he asked if she knew where Rosalie was. Juniper hadn't been paying attention. As they danced, she used her stiletto-enhanced height to look around. The room wasn't so full a person could disappear in the crowd, even someone as petite as Rosalie, certainly not a tall man. "Maybe with Mikhail? I don't see him either."

Dan smirked to show he wasn't perturbed. "Rosalie's going out with me afterwards. We agreed."

Ah, these men, you had to pity their gullibility, but Dan was obviously anxious, leading her to different music than she was hearing. Juniper tugged him from the line of dance and he trailed her out. She'd parked beside Mikhail's car; now his space was empty. She shouldn't have felt the heart pang. Mikhail was saving her the bother of letting him down gently—he wouldn't be another black mark on her conscience. She'd planned to leave him, but that wasn't the same as being left. "I think I know where she's gone."

"Where?"

"Dan, really, let it go."

"You have to tell me."

Juniper ignored the un-Dan-like hardness in his voice. "No, I don't. Forget it."

She urged him inside. He jerked her back and made her look at him. For the first time Juniper saw through his obliging facade to a man who could be steely and unswerving. They locked eyes in a standoff. Juniper was the first to blink.

Dan followed Juniper's car in his own. He wasn't convinced—wasn't allowing himself to be convinced—that they'd find Rosalie at Mikhail's. He'd insisted Juniper check the ladies' room first, but with that they'd run out of options. He'd retrieved Rosalie's street shoes from under the corner table as a favor to her, or as an excuse. He was holding up well, thinking through the situation, driving unimpaired by the drinks he'd shared with Mikhail. He wouldn't accept the treachery as Rosalie's. Even now she must be noting the time, begging Mikhail to take her back to keep her date with Dan. What fraud had he deployed to coax her away?

The entire deception took shape in Dan's mind as he drove: Mikhail luring her to his home in the woods with concern for a fictitious small animal—yes, an abandoned fawn. Dan had no doubt Rosalie would volunteer to calm its trembling and quiet its cries for its mother. The scene was so real to him, he had to remind himself it existed only in his imagination. Still, he continued to think through how it would go: Rosalie would be appalled to learn the story was a ploy. Mikhail would ply her with vodka mixed with something innocuous, but she'd be wise to him by then and refuse it. Dan patted Rosalie's shoes in the passenger seat beside him as though they were living extensions of his beloved. He'd been too humble to name his feelings for her so far, but events had outpaced him. Everything went faster at their age. He'd do it tonight, as soon as he and Juniper extracted her from Mikhail's lair. He switched on the wipers, sudden snow flying against the windshield, just as he'd warned Rosalie it could that warm evening weeks ago. She would learn to listen to him after this.

Juniper had no intention of extracting anyone from anywhere, but she wasn't going to let Mikhail think he'd put one over on her, either. She'd promised herself tonight would be their last time, and it would be, on her terms. Dan's headlights weaved behind her. Whatever was going on with him, he needed to be more careful on the road. They parked behind Mikhail's car in his driveway. The house windows were dark; no one answered their knock, but the door was unlocked. The air inside was redolent with wood smoke. Boris thumped his tail from his bed by the fire and didn't bother getting up. Firelight flickered from the stove. The only other light came through the windows from the hot tub outside, glowing up from underwater, turning the snowflakes into fireflies.

Juniper blocked Dan from barging through the living room to the deck where Mikhail stood, still dressed for tango, his back to them, a glass in each hand. He drank from one glass and lifted the other in tribute to Rosalie, who rose from the water haloed in steam as cold air hit her wet skin, a goddess clothed in radiance and nothing else. She stepped out. Mikhail gave her her drink, drained his, and enfolded her in a blanket—the one that had been Juniper's only days ago. Then he lifted and carried her, laughing, back toward the house. Dan fled with a sound half-cry, half-choke.

Juniper hesitated, seeing him bolt up the driveway to his car. She spun at the sound of the door to the deck sliding open. Mikhail noticed her first. Rosalie looked to see what had killed his laughter. Her eyes widened. She hid her face against Mikhail's shoulder, then turned back to brazen it out. Through the gaping front door Juniper heard Dan's car peel out onto the road. Mikhail staggered under Rosalie's weight, looked around as though he'd like to hide her somewhere. "Hey, Juniper ..."

Juniper lurched out the door. She wanted to stay to make Mikhail squirm, but she'd got Dan into this, and he was in bad shape to drive. The snow was crystalline, melting as it fell, but it stuck enough that she could see his tire tracks. He'd headed right, into the mountains, away from town.

Rosalie's farcical Venus-rising-from-the-sea act showed Dan he'd been wrong again about everything, his delusions patched together with squirreled-away conceptual scraps. He pressed the accelerator, as though he could outrace the bitter knowledge. He'd read cosmic significance into words and events that meant nothing to her. She'd never taken him seriously, messing with him in an offhand way. His courage, in the end, had failed him, a man who'd dealt in danger and subterfuge as a profession but was incapable of reading a woman, or acting on his heart's urging until he was too late. Exhaustion swamped his will. This circus was over. With Rosalie he'd dared to ignore the voice incessantly insinuating disaster. He'd let down his guard that had kept him alive and functioning for thirty years since *that* day. They could all go off-duty now—the voice, the guard, his courage—he was beaten. When he retired, Dan had gladly given up his gun, a nasty, intoxicating thing he'd never had to use except as a threat. It would have been convenient to have now. His exchange with the man on the river trail came back to him. Nature could be terrible, but never evil; he would engage it as an ally.

Chapter Twenty-Six

Perfect Sacrifice

Juniper decelerated once she spotted Dan's taillights. The snow flurries stopped another ten minutes on, leaving thin slush. Dan showed no caution on the slick pavement, fishtailing around the intersection at the Xanadu Falls road. By the time Juniper got to the Forest Service parking area he'd disappeared, his open car door pinging into the night, his footsteps crunching on the viewpoint trail. The dainty buckles of her *Comme il Fauts* frustrated Juniper's urgent efforts to undo them to change shoes. She thrust her phone into her coat pocket and went after Dan in the stilettos, yelling for him to wait for her. She grabbed manzanita branches along the way for balance in the dark. Her heels dug in enough to keep her on her feet. Her eyes adapted as she went, light from town reflecting off the cloud cover and patchy old snow.

Dan climbed over the safety railing to the creek's rocky bank. Before he'd moved west and learned the scale of things, he would have called it a river. Everyone brought their summer visitors to linger in the cool updraft from Xanadu Falls crashing a hundred feet below. Now the snowpack was thawing fast, swelling the creek with runoff. Dan hadn't thought about ice. All winter the falls had been a stupendous frozen sculpture; now the whole creek funneled into a narrow breach melted in the ice at the top. Broken tree limbs jammed there, held by the current's powerful undertow; boulders punctuated a whirlpool that had backed up behind it. The only route to a clear leap into the falls was across those boulders and over the ice dam.

A lesser man might have changed his plans, or given up, returning to his existential prison. Dan's death wasn't to be sloppy. He wouldn't let it be compromised by circumstance. He heard Juniper coming behind him. Good, she would bear witness to his clear intention, the decisiveness with which he carried it out, no secret suicide fueling grisly speculation. She'd tell the others. Rosalie would see it through Juniper's honest eyes, his final message speaking his unvoiced ardor.

His head felt light, but he made the first few yards across a nearly submerged log, like walking on water, out to the irregular boulders. His shoe soles were slick, but the thin leather flexed as his toes gripped the rough, uneven rocks. He moved in a delirium of confidence, the water swirling and clawing at his feet. What could matter when he was on his way to die? Only to do it right. This one final act.

Juniper knew too much about the strength of currents to try to follow Dan, so much more happening under the surface than you can see. She wanted to stop him, but not to die doing it. How was he finding his footing on those rocks in the dark? It would be perilous in daylight. Maybe the darkness helped, hiding the dizzying water. She was afraid to call his name again, to interrupt whatever was carrying him over. Instead, in desperation, she phoned Mikhail.

Dan reached the middle where the water flowed fastest. He knelt there on a broad boulder catching his breath, high on endorphins. He was so close to the falls' spill he could almost touch the branches damming it. If he slipped he'd be trapped among them, drowning certainly, but without fulfilling his final vision—the arcing flight, his body borne by water over the top, the cresting and dropping and final oblivion—an image to haunt his survivors the way he was haunted by his family's frost-kissed faces. He'd had his moment of unwanted fame, his efforts at rescue called "heroic failure," but failure nonetheless. Who knew what he'd been called behind his back? He would atone with this perfect sacrifice.

The water was singing to him in a loud, discordant chorus, but other voices burbled through. He shook his head. Like a ringing in the ears, the voices wouldn't go away. They grew sharper and unmistakably known to him. His boys' euphoric shouts at play in a summer twilight, an eternity to them with no sense it would ever end, even as it passed into night. Dan's recollection granted them, if not immortality, an afterlife. He looped the memory again and again until Naomi's voice overrode it, her cascading laughter that was both rowdy and refined, relishing her own delight, warm beside him. The answering heat around his heart released the cautious corners of his mouth into a smile. He reached his hand for Naomi's, his fingers brushed cold stone. He had closed his eyes to listen. Now he opened them to wild dark water between himself and a light bobbing and beaming from where he'd left land.

MIKHAIL STOOD ON THE BANK BESIDE JUNIPER AND played his flashlight over Dan kneeling on a rock preposterously far out in the roiling creek. "That's insane! How long's he been out there?"

"Half an hour at least, since I called you."

"Look, Juniper, I'm sorry…"

Rosalie shoved past them. Her shriek cut him off. "Oh, my God! He could die out there!"

"I think that was his point." Juniper's tone was

sarcastic.

"But why? Why would he do that? And why didn't you stop him, or go after him?"

"Because he got here before I did, and because I like being alive."

Rosalie was barefoot, wearing a puffy coat of Mikhail's, swallowed in its puffs to her ankles. She dropped it and ran out onto the slippery log in her backless tango dress, shouting for Dan.

"Rosalie, don't!" Juniper ripped off her stilettos, breaking buckles, and went after her. She caught Rosalie poised at the end of the log and forced her back.

Mikhail felt like he was the only adult in a band of foolish children. He was furious at being coerced through Dan's despair. Out of shame disguised as bravery, he pried a long, thick stick from among the flotsam on the creek bank and set off, jabbing it into the creek with one hand for balance, aiming his flashlight with the other. He wore boots with good tread, and his long legs spanned the distance from rock to rock, but he knew water best from immersion in his hot tub, and the going was erratic. He jumped and skidded as icy water filled his boots. The current dragged at his legs. He braced himself against it with his stick, and torturously regained his foothold. He thanked the god he didn't believe in he hadn't dropped the flashlight. Everyone depended on him.

The women watched Mikhail's flashlight beam picking out the rocks, then the log jam, then reflecting from Dan's glasses. It was hard to see what was happening. Juniper kept a tight hold on Rosalie, both huddled under the puff coat, shifting from foot to foot, Juniper more horrified than Rosalie because she knew more about ways to die in water, more about Mikhail. Mikhail's gallantry astounded her, whether it was from the bottle or in spite of it. He hadn't been someone she thought she could rely on. She'd called him reflexively because he was close—or because he was big and some irrational message crossed a synapse telling her *big* meant strong and capable—or just because she was terrified for Dan and wanted Mikhail to comfort her.

She was ashamed now of exploiting his ignorance and his ego, sending him into a place she knew better than to go. One misstep and he could die, one misstep like Dakota's. A simple thing. Why hadn't she learned? She could have called Search and Rescue. It would have taken them longer to arrive, but the result would be more certain. A horrible suspicion lurked in the cobwebby cellar of her mind, that she *had* learned, that a vindictive, angry black-widow Juniper had purposely ensnared Mikhail in this punishment. She slammed a mental door on that depravity, unworthy of her as she knew herself.

Dan saw light bouncing off the water, someone or something approaching. His legs cramped from kneeling on the cold rock. He tried to remember who had stranded him there. A terrible place, yet he felt a peace he'd forgotten possible. The light blinded him. The voice of God bellowed out of it.

"Dan, I've come to save you."

Juniper feared for the lunatic men as they worked their way back. With excruciating slowness, Mikhail helped Dan over expanses he'd skipped across on his way to death. Rosalie's teeth chattered. She shivered in that scrappy tango dress, her hands outstretched as though to haul Dan in by force of will. This rescue was more careless and unprofessional than any Juniper had ever seen. Against all rules and against all logic, no one died, no one was injured, no one was angry, except maybe Mikhail—more from the testosterone overload stirred by his heroics than by genuine emotion—when at last he abandoned Dan to Rosalie's waiting arms and fell into Juniper's.

Chapter Twenty-Seven

Don't Cry For Me

SAGEBRUSH SUFFUSED THE AIR AT THE SMALL airport as Esteban collected his luggage from the shuttle. The snowy mountains glowed ghostly against the pre-dawn sky. Inside the terminal, more travelers than he'd expected at this hour lined up at the check-in kiosks and airline counters, making connections to Seattle or Portland for longer flights leaving at a more civilized time. It annoyed him to have to fly north and west to travel south and east. He'd chosen the cheapest route to Buenos Aires, and cheap meant circuitous, with many layovers and changes. He felt bad about stiffing the Norwegians for the final rent payment, and for leaving the benign white-haired couple in the lurch. He swore someday he'd repay them all. But he'd sacrificed, too. That last moment, as the new owner drove away with his car, had been like losing a dear friend, or at least a partner in crime. He would have enough to live on for a week or so at his final destination while he threw himself on Aurelia's mercy.

It eased his scruples to know he'd given his students their money's worth in class. Even if he hadn't, none of them knew him as anything but Esteban, who was about to disappear, for the duration of his travel, into the *Jason* shown on his passport. It was harder than he'd thought to slip away unseen, though, with what seemed like half the town's population waiting to go through security, and there, at the end of the queue, of all people, Juniper and Mikhail. Bad luck that they were traveling—worse if they were on his flight—good luck they were too wrapped up in each other to have noticed him. How had he failed to see that relationship developing? Esteban took cover behind a column and watched discreetly. It appeared that only Juniper was traveling. Mikhail whispered urgently in her ear, his arm around her waist. Outside the security checkpoint, they clung in an ardent kiss, oblivious to travelers around them.

A flight to Anchorage was called. Juniper detached herself from Mikhail's embrace. She touched his cheek and turned away. Mikhail swiped tears from his eyes as Juniper's substantial shape disappeared through security, her steps eager toward the departure gates. He waited, maybe hoping she would change her mind, then straightened his shoulders and left. Esteban stepped from behind the column. He wondered if his students would continue with tango. For their sakes, he hoped so. Tango was a solace they could count on, one true and beautiful thing.

The End

Acknowledgements

Warm thanks to my writer friends for encouragement, discernment, and editing—Ellen Perry Berkeley, Barbara Jones, Elizabeth Kelly Stephenson, Loretta Slepikas, Nancy Tyler, Celeste Brody, Bob Sizoo and Jana Zvibleman, and to Jana for her patience in taking the author photo.

Thanks also to Larry Jacobs whose persistence over years finally persuaded me to try tango lessons. To Alicia Jumar who guided and shaped my first tango steps. To Tyler Haas and Emma James for generosity in sharing their tango skill and enthusiasm. To the Bend, Oregon tango community, and Argentine Social Tango dancers everywhere.

Deep gratitude to Kevin Kadar, the brilliant artist I was fortunate to meet while dancing to live music of Alex Kreb's orchestra at Portland, Oregon's Valentango.

To Patricia Marshall, Claire Flint, and Cecilia Hagen at Luminare Press. To Willamette Writers.

And to John Kvapil for being there every step of the way, on and off the dance floor.

Kristina Bak grew up in the Pacific Northwest, dropped out of Reed College in 1969, and spent enough years hiking in the North Cascades to graduate from Western Washington University in Bellingham. She explored utopias via Paolo Soleri's Arcosanti and the University of New Mexico. Graduate studies in architecture at the University of Washington earned her a Fulbright year in Rome before she moved to Australia with her husband and six-month-old daughter for three years. Back in the US the family lived on Bainbridge Island until Kristina graduated from Antioch University, Seattle, with an MA in Psychology. They moved to Bend, Oregon, in 1993. Since that time Kristina has worked as a rural mental health therapist, taught Qigong, and sojourned in Sydney as a ghostwriter, among other things.

www.ingramcontent.com/pod-product-compliance
Lightning Source LLC
LaVergne TN
LVHW040145080526
838202LV00042B/3033